Liam's Going

A NOVEL BY

Michael Joyce

McPherson & Company
Kingston, New York

Published by McPherson & Company,
Post Office Box 1126, Kingston, New York 12402,
with assistance from the Literature Program of
the New York State Council on the Arts.
Printed in the United States.
Typeset in Jenson.
First edition.
1 3 5 4 2
2002 2003 2004

Library of Congress Cataloging-in-Publication Data

Joyce, Michael, 1945-
    Liam's going : a novel / by Michael Joyce.— 1st ed.
        p. cm.
    ISBN 0-929701-66-6 (alk. paper)
    1. Mothers and sons—Fiction. 2. College freshmen—Fiction. 3.
Automobile travel—Fiction. 4. Separation (Psychology)—Fiction. 5.
Hudson River Valley (N.Y. and N.J.)—Fiction. I. Title.
    PS3560.O885 L43 2002
    813'.54—dc21
                                            2002007484

Excerpt from "Flowers by the Sea [first version]" by William Carlos Williams, from
Collected Poems: 1909-1939, Volume 1, copyright © 1938 by New Directions Publishing Corp.
Reprinted by permission of New Directions Publishing Corp.

Excerpt from "Suburban Woman: A Detail," by Eavan Boland, from Outside History: Selected
Poems 1980-1990, copyright © 1990 by Eavan Boland. Used by permission of W. W. Norton
& Company, Inc.

This book is
Trudy's and Eamon's
equally, elders

Leavings

I loved you long
before I loved you lost
That I should have loved you less
I cannot say

The cool precision of tomorrow lies
out of reach

and what we look back from beckons
now beyond our understanding

a distant mountain say
or a letter in a young man's crabbed,
excited hand

—CATHLEEN HOGAN WILLIAMS

CHAPTER ONE

Echo

She remembered well the procession of names given to
this place, from echo to butter to storm, though it had
lain in her memory nearly as long as Van Winkle once
slept in mountains nearby. From memory, also, she knew the
light on the fair hairs along the curve of the earlobe of the man
next to her who was not her son then, nineteen years ago, not
Liam whose own fair ears now were plugged with black foam
inserts. Both the mountain and the man she had known from
another life, before the birth of this son, and yet within the life
that had led to it—interludes in the old mountains where light
spilled, hawks rose, memory slept, rain had come, and music
sounded.

A clang of tinny treble seeped from Liam's earphones. She
caught his eye; smiling he adjusted the volume before she could
touch her own ear. He would allow her to mother him during
this journey away from his heart's home through a landscape
which she, increasingly, recounted as a rich and once familiar
though minor portion of her own heart's home. She was taking
her son to his first year of college.

She knew he would not merely allow her to mother him but
that he somehow wished as much for now. He was dear and

strange on this journey, yet not unfamiliar. Called on to describe the feeling, she might have said it is like when you eat some rare variety of apple: the shape and situation are alike but the sensation not the same: a different crispness, an underlying tang of wine and grass. He was her son and acting as such, yet on the edge of being someone else, which both knew they wanted and each knew they ought to savor. Though she, to be fair, knowing better than he.

Called on to describe the feeling, likewise she'd have used that image of the rare apple as perfume from another life. She knew words. Her own name hung like an apple from a dry stem of two words that marked her as someone queer and perishable. She was—in some circles only—"the poet" Cathleen Hogan Williams. That was the introduction: *the poet*, a phrase which at once granted and nullified every young wish that had led to it, making one both meaningless and notable. The poet. The apple. The mountain. My son. A life.

They had spent the night, mother and son, in a Motel 6, despite his earnest protests that she ought to choose a place she liked, a country inn, say, or a bed and breakfast. His father's doing, she knew, though on this trip Liam was willing accomplice. She could hear Noah listing it for his son: Try to convince your mother to slow down and enjoy herself on this trip. Stay in some place with charm. Here's some money to take her to dinner with; order a bottle of good red wine.

"Your father always wants romance for me," she had said. "And for you too, if the truth be told."

Was there a damp pride in the young man's eyes? Something weakened there around them. What was he letting go? Not love.

Wife and son, they each loved Noah, father and husband. Was this so unusual? She supposed as much and, though distressed by the inversion of worrying over the effects of love, she nonetheless hoped it wouldn't cause Liam difficulty later.

She had believed this trip would be less an occasion than a ceremony, so it was a delight that they, father and son, had allowed it to her. As a ceremony it required no romantic setting, and anyway the truth was bed and breakfasts always bored her, while the anonymity of chain motels sustained a distance you could call yourself. Noah loved the smoky hearths and plank floors of inns, or coddled eggs as a paying guest in someone's Victorian kitchen. Self came easily to him, he had always had one, ever would. She loved this. Liam was not so gifted; she loved this as well.

Once they settled into the motel she had compromised about occasion and searched the yellow pages for a good restaurant. Liam was courtly and wore an oversized coat and twisted, skinny tie to dinner. She changed from jeans to a red dress and ordered Chateau Gloria. They were each pleased when the waiter produced two wine glasses without questioning the young man's age. Afterward, Liam solemnly produced a hundred dollar bill to pay the check.

"You?" she asked.

"Dad wanted to be here," he said manfully.

It was very touching; father and son, they each loved her. Was this so unusual? She thought not and yet she wept for Noah's wanting among the litany of things she wept for later that night on a big and empty double bed across from the one in which their eldest and only son slept, his sleeping breath not a snore but a high, sweet music, solemn with dreams and innocent as distant smoke. And although she lay loving what was lost and far away, there was little thought that night of the old mountains ahead or the life she had found once within them.

Liam woke smelling of fear, though he was filled with anticipatory bravado. This next night he would sleep in a wooden loft in an old stone stable made over into a dormitory on a park-like college campus in a quaint town along the Hudson. Some part of its preciousness appalled her, though mostly she was thrilled for him and glad he had chosen this remote and human place rather than a state university with a water tower and an empty wooden stadium looking down on a cindered running track fretted with orange hurdles.

"God, you are weird sometimes," he said.

"Goddess to you, young man," she said and he laughed and let her grip his hand.

If you could not fill your son with images there was no mothering. No poetry either. Still smiling at her vision, Liam slipped the dark foam circles over his ears. She slipped, surprised and pleased, into a memory as fresh as cinders. It was Paul's face, delicate and a little prissy, fair skinned but a lavender sense of stubble under the rosy, ruddy cheeks. God, he was sweet as anything…sweet as apples, and he had hard, strong hands for such a slender man. She felt her loins stir and shifted in the car seat, embarrassed. Lust, too, could wake after sleeping twenty years and crawl up from whatever distant center to make thighs quiver. No Rip Van Winkle this, but some mottled toad-like thing blinking under the dried moss, once wetted back awake, all slime and pebble and not unlike the reptile flesh of sex itself.

She looked quickly, shamed, to see what her son saw. Beneath his eyelids Liam's eyes tocked the muffled beat of music.

A night in a motel, she thought, left her with such feelings. No night more chaste than with one's son, no night more laden. Motels always made her horny and a night of such innocence and expectation heightened it. She liked the word loins but toads frightened her still, years after girlhood.

They were already below Albany when these memories came. It was a Dutch space and ghosted, the green signs of the Thruway announcing the beginning of what was called the Catskills region. The Dutch had believed these hills to be full of strange creatures who overturned ships and lives alike. She had learned these things at the feet—no, not the feet, by the side—of the man with ruddy rosy cheeks and hard strong hands with round knuckles like crab apples.

"God, you are weird sometimes," Paul said.

"Goddess to you," she said and he laughed and let her run her fingers over the round ivory knuckles.

Cathleen, too, had gone away here to college once, though for a summer only and on another campus, yet as quaint and park-like as the one she drove her son toward, and where he would sleep ever after, with brief interludes for Christmases or summers, until his own sons came, or at least a wife filled with images and weirdness, or if not a wife a woman who would love him like his mother did, however sappy or sad he might think her to think so.

Was a wish a thought? She loved driving, how the words looped through you and the road dipped and people swept slowly past, each one turning briefly as you passed as if to assess what life was like in other spaces. Men were better than women, at least in this. They looked on you and sometimes smiled or, when they saw you saw them looking, looked away embarrassed. Most women met your gaze with unyielding faces, watching you watching. Sometimes, she thought, women were monsters of compliance. She glanced briefly at her face in the rearview mirror, no monster but compliant enough, the brief swell of reminiscent lust now lapsed, forehead now (and twenty years ago perhaps as well) dry as bone.

"Shall we discuss the meaning of life?" she asked her son, laughing. He could hear nothing beneath the cushions of melodious noise.

"What?" he said.

"I went to school here one summer," she said.

"Aha," he said, never moving the earphone. He had heard nothing.

"I used to be a ballerina," she said.

"Aha," he said and smiled inside the noise.

"And I rode a silver horse."

"Mom!" he said. He was listening to the music. He hadn't heard her. He wanted her not to bother him.

"Sorry," she said. "Just teasing." He smiled like the men in passing cars.

And if I told you I had a lover here once in these hills would you love me less, my son? If I told you that not long afterward I came back to your unknowing, loving father and that in coming months we joyfully, carefully set off to bring about your birth, would that upset you?

Does it upset me. Did it happen. Was a wish a thought. What are you thinking?

That he spurred me like a horse, slim fingers gripping deeply in the flesh of my buttocks until the bones hurt. How could a thought like this come in the presence of a son. What *are* you thinking? she thought.

Men ask what are you thinking more than women ever do and in a way unlike them. Noah, however, almost never did, and if he did meant nothing intrusive; rather he asked it when he wanted to attend to her and didn't in fact know what she was thinking. On the other hand, at least as she recalled it now (she decided quite consciously to indulge herself in this memory; if Liam could spend these first hours of the day lost in music, well then she could slip for the while into the stream of her own life, ride as well as be ridden), Paul asked after her thinking with more insistence and deliberation than anyone she had ever known. She put it down to his farmer's arboreal soul, wanting to know how things formed and grew.

"Do you think they will read anything of yours in English?"

He had slipped the earphones down around his neck like a stethoscope. The thin sound rung round him and he turned it down but not off. Just as she had slipped into reverie of a handsome man's blue stubble and ivory knuckles along her loins, there Liam was. It had been that way for years. You step into the steaming, placid bath and no sooner has it settled back to a single surface after the ripple of your slipping in than your child is there, a sweet son with questions or demands or a small hand trailing in the still water near your shoulder. She hated how he did this. No, not hated. It was another riding, a gentler, different one. There was no nicer imposition, though it always annoyed briefly before lapsing. O my son.

"I haven't written anything in another language," she said, the joke thin and yet bringing a smile to him like a hand trailing in warm and placid water. "Why? Would it bother you? It would me if I were you, I know."

He was proud of her she knew, knowing from a most surprising source, the so-called personal essay he had written to gain admittance to the campus and the stone stable, an essay in which he had spelled out a genealogy of language.

"From my father, a lawyer, I inherited a sense of the justice of language and how it can sometimes be used against the weak as much as to protect them. From my mother, the poet Cathleen Hogan Williams, I inherited a love of music (though I really am not poetic) and a feeling that language makes you strong."

She did not want to dispute what he had written but she found these words poetic and profoundly moving and had committed them to memory and made them a part of the litany of things she had wept for as she awaited sleep.

"No it wouldn't bother me," he said. "But it would be weird."

"For you everything is weird," she chided. "Weird in what way?"

"Because I know so much," he said, "and to see you there like that."

The fallen aluminum halo of the earphones circled the pulse of his neck, the smooth hollow of the pulse like a primitive sexual organ, smooth and vulnerable and alive within.

"It wouldn't be me," she said. "And you wouldn't know as much. Not the way they will want you to."

They had been through this ground many times and not all of them, by far, of her making. It was risky, to hazard a criticism of schools, and classes, and the ways that poetry was treated on a day so full of expectation. He measured it so and nodded.

"I don't think so," she said. "I'm not that well known, there's not much anthologized. I'm out of vogue."

He wrinkled his eyebrows; she wondered if he knew the word as such outside its use as the title of a magazine. Could she ask? He had his pride and an inheritance of language and they were en route to his future and in the midst of her past. They were in the region of the Ontereas, the Manitou mountains of the sky, home of the old woman the Cloud Weaver, who wove weather from gossamer and cobwebs and morning dew.

They were all out of vogue, she and the mythic Indian women alike, dry women now, sucked dry like cherries left in the sun.

"I'm going to get off the Thruway at the next exit," she said. "I went to school here one summer."

"In New Paltz?" he made the name a joke.

"No, near here, across the river. I was a ballerina and I rode a silver horse."

"I heard," he said.

She spun around delighted, knowing she would never know for sure whether he had heard her miles before or not, but happy with how he knew her.

And did I tell you I had a lover here once in these hills? and that not long afterward your father and I set off to bring about your birth?

Klinkenberg was Echo Mountain, the oldest name for Storm King. Did *klinken* have the low lost sound of memory for the Dutch that *echo* has for us? O who can know what echoes. We learn by immersion.

It wasn't easy to find Route 9 whatever from the exit. He hadn't put the earphones back on and was studying the sorry little road with cheap motels as if it were a wonderland. She remembered something about there being an alphabet of nines: 9K, 9D, 9G, 9W, each going its own way. There was a MacDonalds and she gestured but Liam waved it away and she was grateful. It was too soon past breakfast for him, too suety for her. They made their way down toward the correct nine, this one W for the west bank.

Winken, klinken, and nod.

She hadn't come here to learn Dutch but Italian.

Donna mi Pregha, a lady asks, *viz.*, the poet Cavalcanti.

"Are you afraid?" she asked.

"A little I guess."

"I meant worried, I don't know why I said that. Maybe it's me who's afraid."

He grinned at her. He was a very charming man, this son of theirs.

"It suits me too, I guess," he said.

She knew when not to clasp his hand.

"The road gets better past here, below Poughkeepsie," she said.

"Is that a philosophical statement?" he chided her.

"God, no," she said. "Am I that obvious ever? Do I cloak my instruction in triptiks?"

"Dad does."

"It is hard for him to say what he feels sometimes."

Liam nodded in silence then changed the subject. "What kind of school did you go to here?"

His voice was a tire on a rumble strip, she had gone over the line between father and son. It wasn't a line she was wary about in general, their hours together—she and Liam, she and Noah—sometimes rumbled throughout. It was just that this day everything manly was delicate. There was an edge to his voice, a moist suggestion of homesickness and missing his father's certainty. She would be a cloud weaver, coax and shape this moisture to her own form, more echo than certainty.

"A summer institute in Italian," she said. "I should be able to say *that* in Italian but the language never stuck with me. I loved its music and so it kept floating away. Instead I learned about apples and the Dutch names for mountains. I was very lonely and afraid. I hadn't been away from your father since we married. We were going to try to have a child when I got back."

She had cloaked her history in a triptik, she knew, all up and down and none of the context, nothing for a young man to orient himself with. He nodded a version of understanding, intent on the ceremony of this journey, but his fingers fiddled with the halo of the earphones.

Sometimes language didn't work she wanted to say, but that would make it worse. She knew not to say: you can listen to your music if you want. Donna mi Pregha:

> *In quella parte*
> > *dove sta memoria*
> *prendo su stato*
> > *si formato*
> > > *come*
> *diafana di lume*
> > *d'una scuritade*

~17~

Where it is that memory forms, taking its place like a veil of light formed of a shadow.

This wasn't a good translation, she knew, though she knew it to be a good line. Sometimes language gave you strength even if it did not stick. In retrospect she believed that Noah had wanted her to go away that summer as much or more than she had wanted to. She loved Italy and Italian poetry and wanted to teach it before she had a baby. The previous summer he had gone with her to the poetry festival in Spoleto. They saw a play in which everyone was nude but gleaming with olive oil. They had laughed that night over a bottle of red. They were on the edge of doing well together, with money in the bank, she publishing poems, Noah about to become a full partner, and earnest plans and a fairly naive timetable about when they planned to have their children. In retrospect she believed that she already felt a form of passion seeping away that long-ago summer, like the hiss of a vacuum can when the metal tooth penetrates it.

Their children. Two. One by the end of the following summer, a girl. Another two years after, a boy. Instead, Liam was born the November following the next summer…which was fine, the girl would come. Then, like a veil of light formed of a shadow, something happened to her. There would be no daughter.

She never thought it any more than fate, and certainly not an ironic turn or punishment, though she was often lonely for the girl she would never have. Sometimes she imagined the poems were conversations with her, sad lost things, dry as an unproductive womb. Paul the orchard man didn't see his children. This had been the first private thing she ever learned from him, their first real conversation.

"Are they your girls?" she asked, perhaps the fifteenth or sixteenth day she stopped to buy a piece of fruit or basket of berries from his stand.

The man was often there, sometimes on a green tractor, sometimes in a white teeshirt next to a brown cash register, sometimes in the sunshine. They took to smiling to one another and by the second week he would say "What will it be today?"

Immersion made her wish to float away. She was *sformiata*, badly shaped, unsuited for the language, in Italian the *s*-hiss before a good word served as a curse of inversion, undoing its goodness. The hissing made Cathleen think of old Sicilian women in black dresses. It wasn't the Italian of the black dresses she wished to learn but rather the stiletto smart Italian of Milano, the laughing sophistication of the talk around the Spoleto festival, and the renaissance lushness of Cavalcanti. The idea of the institute was that you would spend all your days and nights in an Italianate manor house along the Hudson speaking nothing but Italian, however ill-formed. You started with the doorknob (*maniglia*, she remembered) and before long: *la diafana di lume.*

Some people learned languages from movies, some from settling down for a month in another country with nothing more than a phrasebook and a radio and the curiosity to wander about a city. Everyone learns at least one language from having a mother and watching her heart's song.

"Will you take German again?" she asked her son.

He hadn't donned the earphones again. She wondered were they each dreaming.

"I suppose," he said. "I have to take the advanced placement. Really I'd like to study Gaelic."

"It's a hard language," she said.

They were moving smooth stones back and forth.

"They have a Celtic society," he said.

"Very new age, I suspect. Wizardry and such…"

"I guess," he said.

His name was Liam. Very Celtic.

Paul knew Italian.

"I learned it from tree men," he had said. "A lot of them are Italian."

For a moment she thought of fairy tales or opera. Norse myth transformed to Verdi. Olive trees with gnarled faces, poor Ariel clasped in a cloven pine. Paul was a simpler man and devoted to his art. He meant what he said. There were Italians who had worked the orchard for him and taught him how to prune and graft. He had sons he no longer saw; the sweet blond girls who worked the stand and laughed with him were people he hired.

"I don't see my children." A strange thing to tell someone newly met. "My wife has them. The last time was once in Kingston along the Rondout. I was walking down the street and she was coming toward me with them. She crossed the street and went up the hill. I haven't seen them since. That was nine years ago."

It terrified her then. She and Noah were going to have children and they would see them forever.

Now forever was interrupted.

She pulled herself from this. Something was wrong. Liam had responded three times in the same voice, a little too lost for her liking, though she didn't know that there was anything she could do for him.

"Something wrong?" she asked.

"Do you know how often you move your lips while you think? It's like you're mumbling to yourself. It's very distracting," he said, "it makes you look crazy."

She would be damned if she would say she was sorry.

"I was thinking of Italian," she said.

"Not always you aren't."

He tried to smile himself out of it. Boys his age, young men, spent extraordinary energy on themselves, she knew. They were self-involved; it was what young men do.

"Poets do that," she said, "move their lips."

"Old ladies too."

Bastard, she thought. Or not that, no, truly your father's legitimate and legitimating son, both sometimes annulling me with good sense and logic.

"Jesus!" she said, steaming. It was too much to think a two day car trip would not have its irritations. And he was anxious about college.

"Sorry," he said.

"Okay," she said.

They were below Poughkeepsie. It would not be long before the road got better. There was another MacDonalds and she gestured and this time he nodded. He was hungry, it made him surly sometimes. They could both be like this, father and son, hunger made them sullen. They longed for red meat. When the breast is gone they devour the mother entire, she thought.

He was hungry. She should have remembered but there was so much else to think of.

❧   ❧

Some people learned love from movies, some from settling down for a summer in another country with nothing more than a phrasebook and a radio and the curiosity to wander about back roads.

Cathleen had learned love long before she came to wander these roads where, briefly, she loved another. Even then she did so in the sense of also rather than instead of, and before long it was over. Noah loved her like no other, she was his heart's song. That never ended and was never interrupted. She wanted nothing when she came here and that, she came to believe, left her vulnerable. It was better to want something.

Now she wanted everything and that made her strong.

Children swam screaming through a hollow pool of red plastic balls before her, their shoes shelved in a red and yellow hive near where their mothers chewed gum and watched each other watching. A rope web swung above the roiling plastic sea guarding the entrance to a jointed white throat, also plastic, which disgorged little girls in crinolines at the end of its slide. Laughter ricocheted like a recording. This was fun in a box, the birthday party and the indoor playground each taking the form of what they called a happy meal. Liam sat with his back to the turmoil, calmly chewing. He took great bites from the triple-decker burger.

"You'll be a vegetarian before Christmas break," she teased. "It's all the rage now."

"All the rage indeed," he teased back. "Where'd you learn that *jar-gone*, doll? American Movie Classics?"

"Who you calling doll, doll?"

Paul wasn't Lady Chatterly's lover, no country hunk or bumpkin by any means. He had attended Cornell not, as she had mistakenly—understandably—assumed, in horticulture but in history.

"They are the same thing," she had said and he thought her wise.

Wise she was, though no doll.

A doll was this girl in a tartan party dress standing dumfounded at Liam's shoulder. She stared at him though he had not seen her. He broke the hearts of six year olds everywhere.

"Hello there," Cathleen said. The little girl smiled.

"Cindy, come over here," a woman called from the group at the party.

Liam dangled a french fry like a worm before her. The woman arrived and stroked the girl's hair gently. Cathleen braced, expecting to hear her son chastised.

"Can she?" Liam asked the woman.

The girl watched her mother.

"Sure, if she wants to," the woman said. He broke the hearts of thirty-six year olds everywhere.

The girl took the french fry and smiled then skipped away.

"What do you say?" her mother called after her.

Cathleen feared Liam would troll a french fry toward the mother.

"Thank you," the woman said to him.

"Doll!" Cathleen teased him as they went to the car.

Who would take him away, she wondered, glancing back at the gaudy restaurant.

She wondered when you stopped looking among the passing restaurants for the ones with the indoor playground. Even now every time she saw a tractor she almost said so to him. He was eighteen years old, going on one hundred, and she searched the highways for cars and trucks and things that go, looked in the sky for shooting stars and hawks and the moon in daylight, wanted to hold him whenever he seemed sad, longed to know any one secret he would tell her.

She wouldn't tell her secret to anyone, but not because it shamed her. Rather, it formed her and was still a wonder (though the truth is that, following that first fall when she thought of it constantly, she hadn't given it as many hours of thought in the intervening years as she had in this one morning). She was lucky enough to know what she loved. Any mother would wish her daughter as much.

Any daughter her son.

"Do you want me to drive a while?"

"Sure, if you want to. But you'll have to save your strength for unloading all this stuff. I'm a frail woman, a poetess…"

"Ha!"

He held out his hand. It was a shock to see it though she knew it as well as anything, having studied his body through the years like she studied the sky for a daylight moon.

She loved Noah through his hands, at first and still. They soothed sometimes and other times rooted. In his profession they cut the air before him and settled in gestures. As a father they cradled and cuffed and caught. As a lover they wandered and gentled, persisted and insisted. She could suck on them for hours if he would let her. They were neither refined (the apple grower had slim fingers) nor slabbed, rather substantial. They had a perfume to them and sometimes sliver moons shone through the dusky broad nails. He never noticed cuts on them, though she always did.

"Well?"

Liam still held his hand out. He was thinking her weird again.

"I was thinking how much I love your father," she said.

"Are you going to survive this trip?" Liam asked, laughing. She dropped the keys into his facsimile of his father's palm and swatted at him with her own.

The other one, the only other lover, made his fingers a tracery and when they made love she imagined he drew thickets on her, vine and bramble, etch and answer, design and furrow, line.

She was only nine years older than Liam is now. Hardly a woman and yet it was a lifetime, older than the girl in the party dress, younger than the mother. She and Paul had only made love twice. Theirs was an *amour courtois*, courtly love, exquisitely brief and so forever.

"Will you be true to her?"

They were talking about his girlfriend Jennie and how it had been to say good-bye to his first true love. He liked to talk about his loves with her; most boys would, she suspected, if taken seriously. It had started as a way to fill the time and to slow him down. She had forgotten how drab the road was below Poughkeepsie and how little of the river there was to spy. She wondered if she would remember how to find the mountain. He kept accelerating through the small towns, in a hurry to be older, elsewhere.

"I mean did you promise not to see others."

It surprised her that she didn't want to see the girl hurt him; a child as blonde as corn silk with round, substantial breasts that Cathleen felt when she hugged her. It wasn't easy to stay true at this age. Jennie had a mouth like a rose.

"Your mouth is like an apple blossom," Paul had said when they first kissed. It wasn't poetic or, given the circumstances, terribly unexpected. Still she liked the symmetry of it, and that a man could attribute paleness to a woman's lips, or that he saw them as a cup.

She chose rather than fell in love and was stubborn enough to think this was the case for everyone despite knowing better and evidence everywhere to the contrary. Even so she chose by littles and fell each time. For her, falling in love was a jagged line, a strobe rather than a firework.

Noah was a faller and so was his son. When she had met him he was very much in love with someone and she approved of that in him. To this day they kept a framed photo-collage of his law school love on a wall in their house outside their bedroom. She too was a lawyer now, and elsewhere, a Christmas card. Cathleen insisted that they neither dislodge what they had felt. He fell for her and she approved of that too but insisted that he treat his two loves equitably. Meanwhile she found herself choosing him.

It shocked her now to think how wisely they had picked their ways through stones that bruised others; and she knew, without priding in it though surely with pride, that she had been wise beyond a young girl's years. It was, she knew, what the educational psychologists called hypercorrection but that any Catskill hausfrau would have known as character. As a poet she was open to the force of feeling and a love for equilibrium, yet a girl who persisted in thinking herself a poet was often treated as a lesser being (though not, you know, by her mother). She wouldn't have it, she meant to mean. It terrified her to think how many right choices she and Noah had made together, though she didn't really fear the wrong ones in retrospect. There were plenty of mistakes; they had been young together and still were. What you remember with a chill is the precariousness of the step, not the tightrope walker's fall.

Even so she thought she must have been a votary of balance, and she saw as much in Jennie. In some sense it was too bad the girl and Liam had met so soon, before life could stick, though god knew and Cathleen knew that it often happened that people thought it had.

She wondered whether it might not have been better had she and Noah been less wise and more bruised. Yet, perplexingly, she could not identify what "it" she meant. Their lives? This day? This losing a son which is not losing but loosing, giving, not away but a way.

Shit, she thought, it was all so cheap. Wordplay annoyed her in herself and others. "A poet of workaday wonder," someone had called her once in print. It seemed a slap, perhaps because it was true. *Sans jeu*, she thought, helpless now, rhyming like a fool.

She was helpless in the car as well. Liam drove like a missionary bringing his presence to heathen space and, because he assumed the driver's seat, he considered the radio and stereo system his space as well. And so she sat in a croon of testosterone and balladic aching. All his tapes were sad British boys with sweet guitars and forlorn lives which, though comic, she was touched that he chose to listen to. He wanted to have a sensibility, but that took experience and he hadn't had enough life yet for that.

He would, she knew, and she ached a little.

Noah was curiously that way when they met, though a full decade older than their son was now and already a member of the bar with three blue suits and five red ties and two identical pairs of black benchmade British shoes. She ached for him as well.

They had talked about the shoes when they first met. Cathleen's and Noah's story was neither one of happening to meet nor one of being thrown together but rather, she insisted, one of choosing to spend the most of an afternoon talking during a rather large gathering that brought many mutual friends of one hostess to a large cottage on Lake Michigan. Probably he was drawn to her because she wore a diaphanous long beach dress and sat in a wooden chair and so seemed safe to someone there without his girl. She had never heard the word "benchmade" and he explained it so thoroughly she felt sure he was repeating what a haberdasher had told him when he'd gone to be fitted out as a young barrister. Even so it was dear.

He had never met a poet though he read poems, good ones too.

"I am not a bad poet," she had told him, "I can't say more. It isn't easy to know whether you are good."

"But what will you do?" he asked, a question like his hands, broadly practical.

"Teach, most likely. Marry. Continue or cease."

She reached for the volume control and eased it back in the constant dance of mother and son at the wheel. The gesture had saved her from a painful memory, one of the Emily Dickinson moments of a woman poet in her twenties. One talked that way then: continue or cease. Liam's recordings were nothing less and no less poignant.

"Think of all the Volvos," she said to Liam, "coming down through valleys and over mountains bringing all the good little children of yuppiedom to college and to life."

Liam laughed with her. He shared her own odd sense of being what they were. On the dromedary dashboard before them nubbly twin humps held matching air bags, soft as clouds, sudden as death. She had a sudden fantasy of sailing off, the bags billowing out like parachutes and, after the first thundering concussion, a noiseless drift down from Storm King and across the Hudson.

(If you wanted to know more about Paul, she could tell you something more about Volvos.)

She and Noah had baked bread that first afternoon, something completely impractical and romantic in a beach house in August. It was an event they marked ever after in any season, but best of all still in the hottest summer.

The pillow of the resting loaf was "like a baby's ass," she said, not really knowing. In her imagination he wore the black benchmade shoes with his nylon trunks and teeshirt. They went down to the water to escape the baking kitchen and she watched him watch as she took off the beach dress and then let him take her hand over the stones near the shore.

He had fallen long before that she supposed but saw it clearly when they returned to the cottage and the smell of dill from the bread. The three loaves were gone in the instant they put them out for the others on the long table on the porch. She and Noah shared a thick crust soaking with melted butter. He wanted to know if he could see her and she wanted to know that also. She could recall the sounds of voices on the beach and in the water and the feeling of her toes on the sand-burnished wood of the deck.

Paul she loved from apple tree to pear tree, apogee to perigee, in a single summer.

Apple tree to pear tree was how the Hudson sailors remembered the tides. Known to the Indians as the water-that-flows-two-ways, the Hudson like all women was tidal and quotidian. Knowing her tides was sailing her.

Somehow one afternoon as she bought strawberries, she began to talk with Paul about the river. There had been several talks by then, sometimes when she fled the dreadful summer institute she thought she was looking forward to them.

"Flood tides are weak when the moon hangs far away in the 'apple tree' and are full when the moon hangs near 'in the pear tree.'"

"So you do know poetry," she said to him.

"Other peoples' poems, yes," Paul said. "That happens more or less to be a direct quote from a very popular history of the Hudson written in the thirties by a fellow named Carl Carmer. The same guy helped save Storm King from the power company in the sixties when Scenic Hudson started."

"Still, you know," she said.

He plucked poetry like apples from where it hung; it made her feel naked.

"I don't know any of yours," he said.

"It isn't useful for history," she said. "Or agronomy."

"I grow apples and peaches and pears," he said. "I'm not an agronomist. I have an old Chevy pickup with rusted quarter panels and not a square Swedish sloop."

He thought her Volvo amusing. "This valley hums with them," he said. "They are like Washington Irving's Dutch housewives, broad in the beam, humorless and practical."

She felt curiously peeved by this teasing. Thinner than that, more mystical. Even so, she was choosing something with him.

"Do you know what happens when two Volvo's collide?"

"No," she said, bored with the boy in him.

"A black hole," he said.

She didn't get it, briefly thought it was something sexual. An historian, he could read her incomprehension.

"A black hole?" he said. "As in astronomy? When energy folds in on itself."

"I get it," she said. "That's very funny."

He was not flustered. He told a story.

"Carmer tells about Peter Kalm, a young Swedish naturalist, who lay one night on the deck of a packet sloop anchored just above what was called Danskammer, den Duyvel's Dans Kamer actually, the devil's dance hall, a huge flat rock above Newburgh where the Indians used to dance in moonlight and frighten the superstitious Dutch—there's a power plant on the rock now. Anyway, Kalm lay on the deck on a June night and watched clouds of fire flies. 'Swarms of the little flying lamps descended upon the rigging,' Carmer says, 'making each rope into a shimmering chain of light.' I always liked that."

Cathleen liked that too, though she suspected the story. It was late June, the season of fire flies, and the Swedish naturalist was too easy a link from the Volvo. Still she could see the blond boy lying on the wooden deck and looking upward at the shimmer of rigging.

Juice ran in her then and she spoke to cease (or so she thought then and until now, now wondering at the ceasing which invites continuance).

"You know that I am very happily married," she said.

"You know that I was unhappily married and I don't question your saying that," Paul said.

She went home to the Italian villa immersed in choices and wishing she could dream of a blond boy blanketed in light. They had not kissed and only barely touched, exchanging coins for fruit or looking at a map. Even so she drove out alone the following night along the eastern bank and down to New Hamburg, a small town where you could get to the river near the yacht club. Danskammer sat on the opposite shore, the factory a fairy land at night with its warning lights and white smoke in moonlight. It was as Paul had said, he hadn't exaggerated, the power plant shook upon the rock and beat a dancing drumbeat. Downriver a little farther the Newburgh bridge was a chain of light and beyond it the shadow of Storm King loomed, limned with silver moonlight.

She chose to love Liam as well. She was still in the midst of choosing. A teenaged boy was a hard thing to love, this she had known from her own teens but perfected in the five years of his. He was, she thought, the occasion of her cloister, a source of solitude, joy, occasional mortification. She had learned to impoverish her spirit from poetry but perfected it in parenthood. With a teenage boy there is constant noise, aural and visual. His hormones scream, his bedroom walls howl with notices of *notice-me*, he leaves behind a wake of light and noise in every room: stereo, TV, lamps and video games all on, phones off the hook, the vacant sound of earphones still tethered to abandoned music. She made silence for herself the way smooth water forms in the wake of a motorboat. In the way she loved him she tried not to hate him.

It was more difficult for Noah, he wasn't monkish. Clerkly, he clashed, collided, shouted, sulked; these were debits. When you add some men to a teenage boy you get two teenage boys. On the credit side were enthusiasms, sports, hilarity, a bully kind of comradeship, vulnerable at root but roaring nonetheless. Loudness increases by male multiplication with a compound rate of interest. She took a vow of poverty. For a while even poetry stayed away and left her alone.

It wasn't all bad. In fact it was good to be alone while you fell in love. It kept the choosing pure.

There was a turn here, she knew, but she could not be certain how. She signaled him to ease off and he lowered the radio. Silence pooled.

"Yes?" he said.

"We turn soon," she said. "For Storm King."

Its oldest name was echo. The silence echoed with the music.

"There!" she said. "Now, 218."

She'd remembered the route number through the years. How some things stick, like music, like love. There would be a turn soon beyond the mustard brick of the military school, an ugly place where teenage boys played football on a field shared with a decommissioned tank, its cannon forlorn as a dog's penis. It made her sick to think of boys educated to this cadence, all randomness and noise marshaled out of them. She would rather learn to love a noisy son, to see him find his own intervals, silences, caesura.

"Am I moving my lips again?" she asked him.

"No, but you are fairly bouncing in your seat you're so excited."

Fairly bouncing was an odd phrase for a young man. She *was* excited. There would be a long curve through a small town called Cornwall on the Hudson, a quiet stretch and then trees and a high chain link gate where the road climbed through shade and up along the shoulder of the mountain into sunlight.

"I love this mountain," she said.

"I see that," her son said.

"There's so much to see," she said. "I want you to love it too."

I will, he said, I will. At first she couldn't tell whether he said so aloud or whether she heard him say so in the silence of her heart and then she was too afraid to ask whether she heard him correctly. Had she imagined it? It didn't matter. That she could imagine him saying it was as good as hearing him say so. She had raised him well, she knew.

I will, he said. I will.

CHAPTER TWO

The Wild Edge

Seventeen in sixty-three puts one where.

Noah had written this out.

If you looked upon the sentence, fully transcribed as it was, seeing it as a mathematical expression rather than short-hand for an adolescent history, it became a series of successive cuts not unlike the endless progression of the values of π. Even in its beginning a cousin: three point seven oh five and so on, ending perhaps never.

Every division is a space for something. This one just missing abrupt closure, one that would have ended all its geometries: on the second cut the seven times seventeen makes one nineteen, just one short of the one twenty remainder.

No, the remainder was one, what was left, and the one twenty was a divisidor or dividend or something, a lost word really, itself a schoolboy history as surely as the sixty-three.

His son and wife were gone, only one to return, at least for now. He remainder.

Noah chose to write out the long division, rather than use a calculator, the seventeen bracketed by the hut of the elder divisidor, that older number huddled underneath the notched hutch and the young man at the portal, next door neighbors.

You could tell a story about anything, even two numbers, using words.

He preferred words for numbers, almost always writing them out despite the rules which stripped away their alphabetical cloaks once they reached adolescence. This was, he knew, largely Cathleen's doing—his wife's influence, indeed their marriage, one of inscription in every sense.

(Oh, he thought, in every sense indeed, missing now her scent and flesh.)

Missing their son, already a dull ache. The one remainder.

Seventeen in sixty three is 3.7058823529 by one accounting. The blue-green numbers peered out from the narrow window of the calculator like immigrants in steerage. Beyond this narrow window there a dark line of similar faces stretched out of sight behind them.

He put the calculator away, it was a horror story, and stared dully at the yellow pad with its runic sentence, working out the calculation.

Seventeen in sixty-three puts me where?

Three sevens is twenty-one and carry two, three ones plus two is five, minus is twelve remainder (the last supper). Bring down a zero (all for naught) is one twenty, times six, no seven is forty nine, carry four, times one is seven plus four is one nine, one remaining.

Three point seven oh five eighty-eight two three five twenty-nine.

Briefly he felt his life like a pachinko table, the silver ball falling through the silver pins and out of sight, a comet of stainless steel.

The phone rang again.

Inside the house were two beepers but the cell phone was with Cathleen whom he had coerced into taking it, saying it would spare him from worry.

"In case," he had said.

"We are only going downstate," Cathleen said, "not down the Zambesi."

Oh the things she could say sometimes, any word with texture eventually latching onto her, like sailors to hookers.

"Which am I?" she asked. "Sailor or hooker."

Only recently she had suggested she might turn tricks for Liam's tuition. A poet in a miniskirt in a subdivision.

"Please?" he had persisted. "For me?"

She should have her own phone now, he thought. Then wondered: to replace Liam?

And to replace me? A vibrator perhaps, he laughed to himself. If so, she was already outfitted and he was a corpse twice over.

"For you I will take survival rations," she said, nuzzling him. "Beef jerky and tricolor freeze-dried Neapolitan astronaut ice cream."

"I wouldn't trust a tricolor jerky," he said. "And be sure to call me on the cell phone before you eat that hyphenated ice cream."

And then they were off and he remained here, alone on a weekend.

He would answer no phones and wouldn't be beeped. He was wasting away a Saturday and, just now, thinking about the French woman.

He rehearsed the things to be done instead of phones. Ride out over the great lawn on the John Deere to the place which, at

Cathleen's bidding, the lawn service did not do. "The wild edge," she called it. In spring trillium followed by violets, sometimes swept over with a sea of yellow mustard, each pulled out by hand. In autumn thistle, lying like a pale lavender cloud where the wetland verged.

Though still August it was autumn already.

What he would do would be to scythe the wild grasses, pull timothy from between river stones, Cathleen away. Leaving the string trimmer up in the shed, the wild edge more suited to ancient tools.

The phone rang again.

It could be Cathleen, it could be them, checking in from the college.

"What a generous thing you have done," she had said when they left, nestling against him, smelling of lavender, her flesh pressed against him. He inhaled the rainy odor of her hair. "To give up this for me," she whispered, "is more than I could imagine."

Her whisper the sound of rain.

"He's the gift and you gave it," he had whispered back.

Liam watched their ceremony, his parents' parting oddly more ornate than his own from his father. Liam was embarrassed by their affection, but also and more recently more and more curious. As if we were elands, Noah thought. Endangered species, the unlikely antelopes from the storybook of Liam's boyhood ABC's, how many years ago.

Seventeen. He was eighteen now, about to be a college freshman. Eland and Gnu and Kookaburra; could a son ever know enough about the creatures of a wild world?

Gone away downstate with his mother, the car filled like a tinker's caravan with stereo and shelving, footlocker and mini-fridge, each division a space for something.

He felt a sudden ache, wishing he'd left something there, a baseball card, a fishing lure Liam would look on and think of him.

A lure exactly, treble hooks sunk in the poor boy's surprised hand. That would be something. Thanks dad.

Even so Noah wished. He felt furtive, wanting secrets, found or left.

He thought of looking in the bedside drawer where there were furtive things, oils, silk scarves, the two small battery powered ivory machines. It was a return to adolescence, a boy alone in an empty house, next thing he'd be pressing her underthings to his face, suffused in the fragrance.

He was lonely and it tugged at his belly, not like a lure but an emptiness, tugging.

Furtively Noah got up and went into her study and looked at the book again. Earlier he had made a discovery and now he looked to confirm it. The phone machine blinked with the new messages.

The John Deere needed new spark plugs. There sometimes was deadly nightshade along the wild edge.

What a wonder this would be for Cathleen, he thought, regarding the French woman. It *was* her, he did not need to study the face on the book again. Even so, he reread the entry from the chronology.

"1963 researched letters and manuscripts of Charlotte Mew at the University of Buffalo library"

There was a book on his wife's desk (a book and a poem, the draft of one) and on its cover the picture of a French woman (herself apparently a poet and writer) whom he (this the discovery he made with his wife gone) knew from long ago when he was a young man on the brink of something, seventeen in sixty-three.

He longed to tell Cathleen this story.

The French woman had smelled of violets, intruding upon them on the warm night, the two boys drinking beer among the ruins of the Corinthian marble columns stacked in the fringe of pine trees on the rise above the lawn which led to Main Street.

"Bon soir. Hello," she said, unfazed to come upon them, as if she were used to fairy tales. He would always remember her voice. This took place in the time before nights turned dangerous forever and a French woman could safely think of sitting herself down beside two boys who were drinking beer on a summer night in Buffalo watching stars and passing buses and thinking of what little they could imagine of the future.

"May I seat?" she said in her accent and Pete laughed aloud. They hadn't heard French accents except from Madame Albert, the librarian and French teacher, and had almost never seen a woman (she was surely a girl then, Noah knew) so beautiful.

"Beer?" Pete said and gestured toward the six-pack nestled in the cool pine needles.

"No thanks," the woman smiled, the accent almost gone.

It was the strangest thing ever. ("Remember," he would tell Cathleen if he ever told her this story, "the sixties had hardly begun as yet.")

"What a magical place!" the French woman said in a voice that sounded like laughing.

He and Pete had thought little about magic in those days, perched to depart for college in what really was to be their last weeks as friends, though they had no way of knowing that and would leave off their friendship that summer for no reason except trajectory and history. Big Pete Ehmer heading to Indiana to try to be a tight end in the Big Ten; Noah heading only a little east and upstate to a college not much different than the one downstate where Liam went now in the company of his mother.

It was different then. The truth was that in those days, and unlike his son, Noah had been heading to a photograph in a college brochure and not a college exactly, the photo a building of heaped stones covered with ivy, and yet romantic as a castle. Another photo he remembered well was of women with long thighs standing holding tall oars at their sides, ends curved like palms. Ladies' crew, it was called that then. He recalled the faint, strange eroticism of the photos, how he had longed to be in a place of such Amazons and stones.

He had not visited, it wasn't done then as far as he knew (as far as his parents knew). Liam's search had been an odyssey of campus visits, Amazons, stones, all of it tied up in obscure formulae: SATs of fourteen twenty put one where?

It was easier in the past before they knew how everything was tallied and accounted.

The French woman perched atop an upturned capital, her bare feet swaying in sandals, a pastel cotton dress the color of daylight. She was the most beautiful woman he had ever seen and now she appeared (just as beautiful in a photograph whose soft-focus approximated memory) on the cover of a book in

Cathleen's study, thirty-plus years after, her feet still swaying in memory, the smell of pines and cigarettes and summer night.

Ghislène Fatoux, a name you couldn't say. He never knew it then but he recalled vaguely that she may have called herself Helen.

Pete smoked a Lucky Strike and traded her one for the blue Gauloise, leafy and licorice smelling. The cigarette was still exotic then, a year or so before Noah would really know these cigarettes from the film society showings of Godard films with Jean Paul Belmondo crosscutting Paris streets.

Ghislène Fatoux. Noah had a dreadful French accent, Liam and Cathleen laughed when he ordered Beaujolais. (Noah hoped Liam had succeeded in getting her to have a good dinner the night before.)

It was a good enough story without knowing the French woman's name, good enough without finding this link through a book to Cathleen.

The answering machine was there, that was his excuse, though he didn't need an excuse to sit in her study (she sometimes let him sit there and watch her think, she loved him so) and in fact had rambled all morning through every room, missing them like a dog misses his masters, by scent and sound, by longing. Covering ground.

The poem troubled him a little. Reading it like this, with her gone and the poem clearly only just begun, felt like eavesdropping or worse, voyeurism, watching someone naked through a window. It made him hurt a little too, a feeling like jealousy, but again through a distant window, not certain of either what you see or whether what you feel is right.

The beginning was especially troubling .

I should have loved you less
I cannot say
I loved you long
before I loved you lost

It made him a little jealous really. Any man had jealous times, especially one who traveled, whose wife traveled. There were times when she gave readings at some college and she would call and tell him about having dinner and drinks with someone and her voice had the lilt of someone flirting at a party, the laughing tone she got after drinking wine.

"Loved you long" made him ache unreasonably, it was the language of sex, though he wondered whether you weren't supposed to read it as "loved you long before."

Seeing her handwriting made him ache a little as well. He inhaled the scent of her study: books and faint, faint perfume. Could he truly be this lonesome after one night and a morning? Or was it something else he missed? He knew it was Liam most likely but looking at the poem it felt like he was missing everything he had ever lost.

Cathleen was feeling the loss, he knew.

He looked at the poem again.

After those first lines one line of a new stanza floated alone:

The cool precision of tomorrow

She had crossed out a second short line with only two words "a globe" and below that repeated the floating line again but this time as part of a stanza:

The cool precision of tomorrow
the equilibrium of an apple beyond
the reach of the picker whose shadow
falls intertwined with that of the tree
in the sun

But then she hatched those last three lines out, the crossing-out a lattice big enough to see through, and then wrote three other lines, below the crossed out ones and indented a little, sitting out from the rest of the poem like a boat not yet in its dock.

her own body and the tree's spare
limbs intertwined, akimbo
in shadow

The last two lines were about Liam he was sure although that made him feel no less jealous or voyeuristic. These lines she would never change.

and what we look back upon beckons
now beyond our understanding

Cathleen and Liam would be well on their way now after the first night's short drive and the night in the motel, maybe to Poughkeepsie or whatever that town was where she had spent the summer learning Italian before she was pregnant with Liam and Noah became a full partner.

The phonecall was from Antoinette Ryan. Two calls in fact.

The first had been a standard message: sorry to bother on the weekend, can you please so on and so forth. The second had an edge of eccentricity.

"Something is wrong with the light," she said. "There is no one else to call."

He could not help but think that in this curious message she was asking him to do something in relation to her painting. She was a painter of minor repute, though from a moneyed family and successful enough to have to decide upon a trust before her death. It was what had brought her to him. Well into her eighties now (one into eighty will not go), she was harp-backed (was that the word?) with what Noah supposed they would call papery skin, her face in spots blotched red as a puppet or better still one of those transparent women they showed in Liam's biology texts.

He imagined that she might have awoken a little confused this morning, went out (as he would soon ride out on the green tractor) to paint watercolors or whatever, found the light milky or dim and, addled, called him. There really was no one else, Noah knew, now that the caretaker and his wife had moved. No relations other than a dull-witted, far-removed great-grand-nephew, offspring of her dead brother's dead wife's sister. The great-grand-nephew lived in a trailer in the red clay South with his fat wife and infant, none of whom she ever saw or heard from. In fact she thought they might not know she existed.

He realized that something wrong with the light could also be how someone spoke of having a stroke. And so, protesting inwardly, feeling unjustly virtuous, he called her.

And reached her machine, thank god.

"Antoinette," he said, curiously calling her that for almost the first time, "Mrs. Ryan, this is Noah Williams. I'm concerned about your message. Please call me back soon."

Still burdened and virtuous he clipped a beeper to his belt and, after one more glance at the picture of the French woman, made his way through the garage and past the Lexus and the open space where Cathleen's Volvo usually sat and took the plastic tarp off the John Deere, piled the scythe and hand tools in its small trailer, and, surprised that it started on the first try with the bad sparks, took off.

He was halfway to the lower lawn when he realized that it was not necessarily a cause for relief that Mrs. Ryan's machine had answered.

The great and lower lawns were joke terms really. Something between Cathleen and him, a disbelieving thing really. They did well enough he had to say when anyone asked. Five thousand square feet on three levels and two lots, three point seven acres, twice the standard one and a half, some in trees. Space enough to justify a tractor, enough for wildness at the edges, though nothing like the great estate where Antoinette Ryan's light failed her and where, Noah increasingly understood, he would soon be heading if he did not soon hear from her.

Jokes aside, because of the drop between the great and the lower lawns he had to steer the John Deere along two hairpin switchbacks, gentle enough but a compounded distance nonetheless. In the first years there they had tried a pond in the lower lawn, a little thing only large enough to tempt a pair of waterbirds and to house croakers in the spring. Perhaps even stock it with a few small iridescent flecked trout.

He had walked the toddler Liam down to see the yellow backhoe, back hoes being among the heroes of another storybook, one devoted to things that go, a book that began a lifelong (Liam's life extending, now that he was past such concerns, into their own since he and Cathleen could not quite break the habit) ceremony of announcing the sighting or passage of just about any kind of conveyance from firetruck to amphibious car to construction crane.

In springtime the pond was supposed to fill from snow melt and runoff and thereafter be sustained by a small spring. It filled just once and drained by June. The contractors suggested a clay cap, an expensive earthworks that sounded not much different than a natural bathtub.

"A place has a self," Cathleen said and they had the thing filled back in. It became a garden on account of the drainage.

Their first month there he heard her on the phone with her mother describing the trees on the property. "Oh, I'd say about two hundred feet tall," she said earnestly.

They were mythic trees, the great oaks perhaps fifty or sixty feet, but nowhere near—no trees save the redwood anywhere near—two hundred. Still he knew what she meant and loved the way her voice sounded.

Trees as tall as a storybook, once upon a time tall.

Antoinette Ryan had a storybook estate, complete with a small lake whose shores she shared only with other estates and, just beyond her house, a drained and ancient concrete swimming pool whose walls were mossy as the churchyard of the poem Cathleen had dragged him to in England once.

Mrs. Ryan and her brother, a fellow named Mulvey, made a fortune in hotels. Mr. Ryan spent as much of the fortune as he could but died young. He wanted to manufacture aircraft.

The poem was by a clergyman named Gray.

He knew poems well enough, had to, wanted to for Cathleen, but wasn't, as one poet who Cathleen was fond of once phrased it, "given to poetry."

Given to her though, he thought, given to the poet as others are to poetry.

It was something the French woman had wanted to talk about, he remembered. "Do you love poetry?" she asked them in the midst of a long talk about school and life and the future. "What do you love really? Do you love anything?"

It was impossibly romantic that she asked that, he remembered. By all rights and given who they were then, they should have laughed aloud. It should have (would have with the girls they knew) set them off into a series of mocking taunts and mooning pantomimes.

oui oui oui je t'aime la poetry

Ha.

But it did not.

She had begun, he recalled, by asking them about the curious ruin where they sat, the deconstructed columns of white marble gleaming like cylinders of moonstone, a collection of ghostly six-packs on the small rise at the edge of the campus. These architectural elements were the relocated colonnade of an old campus building torn down by Rockefeller as part of an expansion that would soon turn the old campus into a professional quadrangle. The master plan was to move the main part of the university into a set of suburban towers along a Thruway spur between Buffalo and Niagara Falls. There the marble colonnade would be recreated in the midst of the newly constructed brick and concrete desert. Rockefeller was doing the same thing then in the state capital, building an empire of white towers in a huge plaza in the gouged and leveled center of Albany.

These were the days before strip malls, before nights turned dangerous forever, and when history was still possible. Like Alexander the Great, Rocky wanted to build great plazas of learning and government where people could see themselves in scale, tiny before all the wonder.

First, though, he had to tear a more comfortable world down. And so the columns had been neatly sawn crosswise into six foot sections and stored under pine trees awaiting history and the two boys who sat there in the company of the French woman.

"How funny, how wonderful, you Americans are!" she had said. "You build new museum to save your past."

She addressed Noah directly.

"Do you wish you were rich as Rockefeller?"

He did not know then, or for years after, that it was a song lyric, and when he found out that it was he realized she had been quite droll back then and he found himself wishing, as you sometimes do, that he could go back in time and tell her that. Only that. How droll you were.

How beautiful.

There was another song from a time nearer that time that was more like their brief encounters. We would have given her our hearts but she wanted our soul.

Don't think twice, it's alright.

In retrospect he suspected, having lived now with a like woman for eighteen years, exactly his age when they had met the French woman, what she wanted exactly, to the extent that she wanted anything exactly, was to elicit the thought that came after the first thought. She wanted to capture the reflection in a mirror after someone has relaxed a pose. In that sense she did want their souls.

Such women did. Cathleen did and it often made him wish he had one to give. Beneath it all he was empty he knew, not self-sorry, not (not at all, really) unsatisfied with what he had become. If he felt himself unjustly burdened with virtue, it was virtue nonetheless and he did feel satisfied (a dangerous word otherwise, he realized) with his own integrity and with who he and Cathleen were in their marriage and with what Liam was becoming and, even as he left them, with what he would likely continue to become. What Noah saw sideways in the mirror these days was a good man of normal features but soulless.

Beneath the surface he was empty. This wasn't an idle or unconsidered assessment. He had tallied it up not more than a week before after a curiously moving conversation with Liam, retreating in a self-sorry and despairing funk to his car in the dark garage, sitting there like a fool with a bottle of bourbon, worried to death by all he did not know about life.

Cathleen found him. She always found him in his darknesses.

She knocked politely on the window and his heart leapt although when he zipped down the electronic window he could do more than look dolefully up at her.

She did what she often did in the darkness around them, distracting him with some question (about water he remembered) and flirting with him like a girl.

At first the back light from the door to the house had masked her features and kept her in silhouette, but when she closed it off the darkness gathered and she took on her own light, her features the moon's face. He had felt, absurdly, the stir of an erection.

"Want a seat?" he asked and patted the passenger-side leather.

How funny it would be to neck in the car like lost teenagers.

She shook her head no. He was drinking the bourbon from one of their cut-crystal whiskey glasses and he offered her a taste. There was a time when they first married when they would have whiskey together every evening, just a sip, and talk.

Her lips on the rim of the glass were tender, the bite of the whiskey crimped her eyes ever so slightly and her bosom shuddered with satisfaction. She looked at him and silently wondered what was wrong.

He knew he would have to explain though he also knew she would not ask him to give too much more than he wanted to.

He tried to explain how he wished that he had another life within him, one where he could confront the questions which seemed to slide by him like ice floes on a dark sea, but the whiskey slowed the words. Suddenly he felt as if he would cry.

She looked on him with lonely love and he felt its suffusion.

We have been married a long time, he wanted to say, it is a comfort.

Instead he blurted the question of Liam's not really a question but a protest which had thrown him into this darkness and left him with nothing more within than the burning reflux of a whiskey depression and a lonely feeling of coming loss.

"It makes me angry and frustrated," he recited Liam's words, a gesture of forefinger and thumb putting quotes around it for Cathleen, "when I think that what we are as individuals might not exist after death."

Liam's careful phrasing had made Noah mournful though he didn't know whom he mourned.

He had told Cathleen a long story about seeing Liam once on a baseball field and how happy it made him. But he could not bring himself to say how the memory of the boy in the fading light now made him despair.

"Do you love anything?" The French woman had asked years before and, his own son's age then, he did not know how to answer and for an instant then too all the world suddenly gaped like a dark cavern within him.

He would have said his family, his mother and father. Even had he not been between girlfriends he knew enough not to say that he loved some girl, knew the French woman was asking something deeper even than mother and father.

Actually his first instinct had been to wonder whether she was some sort of pervert. They were raised to find perverts, hitch-hiking (in the days before hitchhiking, too, was dangerous) they rode with a hand on the door handle and monitoring the driver's conversations for talk of girlfriends or any hint of physical reference. Likewise in their prep school locker rooms they looked on certain classmates with a practiced wariness about softness and ambiguity.

Liam had friends with earrings, male friends, a shortstop and a drummer, though he wore none himself, at least not yet. And from his mother Liam learned another sense of softness and ambiguity. Noah, too, tutored himself in it, seeking it with an insistence not unlike the longing he often felt for the clasp of her embrace and the swift descent into undifferentiated flesh and darkness.

"Do you mean the kind of love that takes you over?" he had asked. It was a question for a question, and it seemed to please the French woman.

"Ooo la la! Tell her loverboy!" Pete hooted.

"I love sometimes how when you hit a baseball it seems to rise into the air like a planet with wings, slowing down so you can see the stitches turning and the splotches of sun on it. Is that what you mean?"

He had been very proud of saying this, almost as if reciting lines of Catullus in Latin class. The French woman had clapped her hands with a delight which shut up Pete before he could mock the goofy poetry of what Noah said.

"Who can say what one means?" the French woman had said with a smile, her eyes piercing the night and him, her bare feet still swaying.

The dark cavern had receded but only to a horizon.

He reached the lower lawn and the wild edge and stopped the tractor, thinking suddenly maybe he should have left it running in case the fouled spark plugs would keep it from starting.

It was a crazy thought, he knew, to bank all the noise of keeping it running against the possibility of a misstart. In the silence left behind by the choked motor there were already bees and the trill of birdsong, the poinging sound of someone hitting tennis balls not far away. Saturday.

11:00 A.M. to 2:00 P.M.	Freshmen Arrive
2:00 P.M. to 3:00 P.M.	First Week Overview (students only)
	Frequently Asked Questions (parents)
3:00 P.M.	President's Reception (all welcome)

In some part of him, despite what she saw of it as his gift to her, Noah was deeply grateful to Cathleen for taking Liam through this apportioned parting. She saved him from the pain which these hours marked, the pain of losing without being able to say so.

"We all love what we see going away from us," the French woman had said. "It's what's meant by mortality, by being alive. Living is loving and loss, isn't it?"

He would remember that always; it was among the few memories from that strange time which he recollected at one time or another to Cathleen. The French woman's phrase had stuck with him, partly because the way she said "living" at first sounded like "leaving" or "leafing."

Leaving is loving and loss. Leafing is loving and loss.

They called the session for parents Frequently Asked Questions. The language of computers had even grown over the old stone campus of Liam's new college like a renegade ivy or what was the vine taking over the south like a mutant movie? yes, kudzu.

Loosestrife north and kudzu south. There was a march of loosestrife along the margins of their gated suburban enclave, a thin purple line through the gully just beyond the community center where someone poinged tennis balls through the sunlight, the line stretching along the low ridge which bordered the westward properties and then spreading over the draining lowland of theirs. Loosestrife was one of the forces one fought along the wild edge. Loosestrife and mustard and grape vine and thistle.

It was a surprise how vines could find any hint of wall. Along the back edge of their property a wire fence remained where the subdivision backed up against what was left of the old farmland which had been sold off to form it. Nothing pretty about it, farmland or fence, the latter a mostly rusting wide wire mesh strung between once green, now mostly also rusty, metal fence posts with tab ears where the wire slipped in, one or two of the posts rusted clear through and dangling there from the wire mesh like broken teeth. This whole rusted and woebegone structure jungle lush with green gone already scarlet and yellow in patches where autumn was slowly settling in.

They left the fence alone, a wall of green now where the vines puffed it. A place has a self. What Noah would work on would be the place where long ago Cathleen had lugged the river stones. The river, or what river there was still, was beyond what was left of the farmland. On a good day you could smell it there, slightly muddy smelling, toadlike, grass scented likewise. There were fish there also, sunnies and smallmouth and finger perch. When Liam was little they had caught them.

Cathleen's stone marked where giants walked, she'd told the child Liam and his father. Polished flat slate black smooth oval footpads.

"Maybe we should chisel lines of your poems into them and paint them gold," Liam had teased her years after, "Like the garden catalogues."

She wore a wide brimmed straw hat with a mosquito net that draped around her face and neck like a silk cloud.

Goddess. No, she would correct him, only a woman. She feared deer ticks, Lyme disease.

"It sounds so pretty, Lyme is a place in Connecticut."

These small things, not the ticks themselves but the microbes they bore, could settle in the heart's passages, the bone caverns of knee and hip, shoulder and elbow. Weigh you down or slow you, cripple or kill you.

The beeper buzzed against his hip and Noah realized he had already missed one call on the ride down here, the vibration of the tractor canceling out the vibration of the beeper. Both the current and the last calls were from Antoinette Ryan. That she had called twice was both a good thing (since it meant she was most likely not having a stroke) and a bad thing (since it meant he would not be able to work here long before heading back to call her).

Would not be able to work here at all just now, he realized. Something is wrong with the light. There is no one else to call. It was not a message you could or should walk away from.

Though he had to walk back. The tractor, predictably, would not start again. It was better actually, to leave the tools down there for later after he'd called her. Go out and pick up some new spark plugs after Cathleen and Liam checked in. Saturday poinging, loosestrife in a slow course along gully and hedgerow, lush things climbing along the fence of memory.

There had been a total of three conversations with the French woman. Either three or four, he could not remember exactly. Though for sure no more than four. The first night and another night after that each by chance (at least on their end) took place in the same space of the tucked away colonnade. A third time by appointment (on his end) took place in sunlight and was unlucky. He kept thinking there was another meeting. Felt certain. Remembered or supposed, wished or imagined.

On the night of that first meeting what was best was how little had happened, how much like any night it was. He and Pete drank beer and answered her questions or watched the night in silence. She smoked cigarettes and laughed and once in the midst of a long silence sang a quiet song, so low they could hardly make out the words which were in French anyway and something well beyond Frère Jacques or their two years studying with Madame Albert.

It didn't matter. It was a pretty song without knowing what it said, pretty and sad, sweet and mysterious.

They asked her what she did and she said it was a question only Americans asked. They asked her what she *wanted* to do and she laughed, a nice laugh but one which made Noah at least feel foolish.

"So you get your wish after all," she laughed again. "How very American. One has to answer your first question by answering the second, *n'est ce pas?*"

"*Oui, vraiment*," Pete replied impressively, although his singsong French made her laugh again.

Noah's memory of that first encounter was filled with laughter, like remembering a carillon.

"I'm a professor. There," she said and laughed, "is that enough?"

He and Pete said nothing. She was too young.

"Or I want to be one," she said.

That was better. They didn't want her to lie to them.

"Or maybe I don't at all. I want to be a writer. I am one. *Oui, je suis*," she said.

Up to then she hadn't seemed real to him. He turned to look at her.

"But what do you *do?*" he asked.

"Do you mean the kind of doing that takes you over?" she asked, smiling at the symmetry.

Noah nodded.

"Well I'm not certain yet, do you see? In some sense that is what I am here to find out. I am researching something which may perhaps become a great study of the greatest writer ever."

She pronounced the word as "some*sing*" like a movie; it was curious to hear someone say what they were doing might become something great.

Noah suddenly had an idea. In retrospect it wasn't much of one and almost certainly prompted by the French woman's own symmetrical paraphrase. Even so for perhaps the first time ever in his life he was borne up by a great daring, an elemental persistence of a kind he had come in his adult years to recognize as the hallmark of the few people he could recognize as having what might be called genius. His wife for instance, and lately now his son as well. The genius of saying the obvious, even persisting with it.

"But what do you *do?*" he asked again.

"Aha!" she said, and he felt it confirmed. "You are wise beyond your years."

"Bullshit," he muttered.

"I'm sorry," she said.

She had hurt him and she knew it.

He had thought the idea was persistence but its name was patience.

"I should not have mentioned years," she said. "Even so, like the apostle Peter, after three times I do understand your question."

It took Noah a second or two to understand how Saint Peter's
denying Christ three times could be understanding a question
and when he did he felt a thrill like a breeze, as if ideas were real
and people lived through them (or in them, he couldn't be sure).
It was a thrill he was used to a little—he and Pete had really
been deep in ideas, or at least dreams, when she came upon
them—but it was a feeling which up to then he thought furtive,
something generally kept to yourself and hidden away outside
the world of women and men except for a certain few occasions
fueled by beer or music or by something like love.

Years later he had wooed Cathleen unwittingly with the same
question, felt the same thrill like a breeze as they fell in love on
a summer beach where they had slipped away from someone's
cottage. She had said she was a poet.

"But what will you do?" he asked.

"Teach, most likely. Marry. Continue or cease."

"Continue or cease" caught him like a dream.

He had thought life was patience but its name was persistence.

"What I do," the French woman said, "looks like reading but
is more like dreaming aloud."

He remembered that phrase, "dreaming aloud," his memory
opening now in a rush as he neared the house and prepared to
call Antoinette Ryan. His previous annoyance at what he might
not be able to get done was now supplanted by something more
like fear, that the memory, like a line of argument, might slip
away like contrails in the featureless blue air.

Mrs. Ryan answered the phone on first ring.

"Thank god, Mr. Williams, thank you for your concern."

Despite her advanced age her voice had the certain kind of patrician strength you associated with the word dowager. It was throaty and almost whiskey rough but still melodious and without that singing-to-oneself quality some old women get.

"You must think I'm foolish with that talk about the light," she said, stopping him from feeling exactly that.

"Well, yes and no," he said. "Whether I can help at all depends on what you mean by light."

"Lux veritas?" she asked.

"What's that?" he asked before he realized and laughed, "oh, yes, that…" he said.

"I wonder if I could induce you away to look at a more sublunary light for me? Your family would be welcome to join you. Perhaps your boy would like a swim?"

"My boy's gone away to college," he said, almost shocked to be passing on this news for the first time.

"Oh my, your poor wife," Mrs. Ryan said. "What can she be feeling?"

"She's taking him there today," he said.

"Well, poor you then," Mrs. Ryan said. "I don't feel half as bad about dragging you away now."

"What is it though?" he asked.

"Light," she said.

"Light?"

"Bulbs and such. Light. None of it works."

"Have you checked the fuses? Did you call the power company?" Noah asked.

"I've called you," she said.

"Yes you have," he said and left not long thereafter.

෧෧   ෧෧

Pete Ehmer died in a car crash in Indiana in October of his freshman year. For a while Noah wondered if there was any way to let the French woman know. It was madness, he knew, but Pete's death was his first.

It was an unspectacular crash, a clear and sunny day in October and a car full of student athletes not speeding, no one drunk, no mechanical failure. A car in an oncoming lane crossed the median for no apparent reason. It was in the days before seat belts. The other driver and Pete both died, the five boys in the car with him survived though some played no sports again. It was in the papers because they were football players. Perhaps the French woman had seen the story and remembered.

Noah joined several although surprisingly not that many of his classmates back for the funeral. People were in their first months away at college, some few had already gone away to the army in those quiet days before Viet Nam was a name they all knew. Some even had gone to work, still at that time not completely as surprising an outcome for a prep school graduate.

Pete looked alive in his coffin. Just a little pale and made-up around his face although little purple whiskers showed through the powder at his cheek. His hair was as always the color of corn silk and his huge hands, so large he could palm a football, were crossed at the second button of his suitcoat and a big wooden rosary from his German grandfather was threaded through his fingers. At the end of the rosary a silver Christus huddled on his cross under the half-roof of a Black Forest hut. Pete's mother hugged Noah and the tears left a wet circle on the shoulder of his suitcoat and the perfume did not go away for months.

"I would die for my grandpa," Pete had said bravely that night under the pines.

Noah could not remember whether this was before the French woman came along. They had talked of death before her and after.

"He came here after the First World War and he worked on the railroads to feed his family and all he wants now is for each of us to go to college. I'd die for him," Pete said.

"I'd die if someone was hurting my mother," Noah offered (he was fairly certain now this was before the French woman). He felt certain that his own offering had seemed as weak then as it did in recollection, an afterthought, more sentimental bravado than Pete's sincere dedication.

"I have no country to die for," the French woman said when the question came around again and they asked her.

"I mean I don't know which country is mine any longer, the one of my birth which has stolen my birth from me, the one of my youth which has stolen my youth from me, the one my body now inhabits without any borders and which threatens to steal my body from me. Anyway 'to die for' is a concept for boys excuse me, *pardonnez moi* for the male. For the woman the concept is to live for. Even to die is to gift of life."

It was all very mysterious, this talk of stolen birth and youth and body. This was partly why they weren't angry, or at least Noah wasn't and he didn't think Pete had been either, when she said the thing about boys. They didn't think then she was talking about them, they knew her by now. Partly they weren't angry because they knew her by then.

What, if anything, did Pete Ehmer die for?

It was more than Noah's first death, it was his first taste of fate and the undeniable tang of its mystery.

These days car crashes were the major cause of death for young men Liam's age, car crashes and suicide.

Liam's first death had come earlier, his grandfather and then two classmates, one car crash, one suicide, neither close to him, though still he had written a terribly moving essay for his advanced placement English course about the latter.

Four people in Noah's graduating class died in Viet Nam.

The French woman was the first person he had ever heard utter the name of that country. She had called it indo-sheen at first and they couldn't hear the name as Indochina, *Indochine*.

"Viet Name," she pronounced it, the accent coming and going in the night like the smell of the pines.

Even to die is to gift of life, she said.

"*Ma famille* is from ail-zhe-ree," explaining she rhymed. Ail-zhe-ree was Algeria.

"They have been torn from their womb. I have, we all have."

The government of Diem fell in a coup a month after Pete Ehmer's death, an event neither Noah nor anyone he knew had marked.

Liam studied Viet Nam as if it were ancient history.

"How did you stay out of the war, dad?" he asked, not "What did you do in the war, dad?"

"Beat the draft," Noah said. "We called it beat the draft."

"Whatever," Liam said, that word which dismissed every difference and so pissed Noah off.

The idea of fatherhood was patience.

"Like most everyone I went through a series of deferrals and then I was going to just go to jail, refuse to step forward and go to jail, but Nixon came up with the lottery and that was that. My number was in the high two hundreds. He had divided the whole movement with lottery numbers. It was long division and all politics went away with the remainder."

Liam longed for these things from him, a sense of the slipping world, the world which was already growing ever more dim before Noah even as it brightened into detail for his son.

To die for is a concept for the male.

"Then why do we live?" Liam had asked a week ago.

It could have been a car crash, the conversation, the way it snuck up on them. They were zapping through channels together and (despite Cathleen's wariness about so indulging their underaged and yet would-be manly son) drinking beer, all very father and son, all very full of deferral and a constant and dull awareness of what could not be said in an impossibly compressed week. Suddenly (improbably) Liam lingered on a documentary about the Grand Canyon, a shot of the wind-rushed swoop of a red-tailed hawk giving way to a helicopter sweep in silence over the landscape of the Kaibab, the Indian name for a mountain upside down.

Liam spoke from the silence, the canyon inside the electric box suddenly like a vortex in their family room.

"Have you ever wanted to be at some point where everything made sense," he asked, "where all your questions were answered?"

It was a monumental question prompted by a monumental place.

On the screen before them the canyon echoed outward in silence, in forms of space which had the sense of unheard sounds.

"What if there was a place after death?" Liam asked, "a place like that?"

He sipped his beer meditatively but did not look at his father.

"That's why I'm going to do astrology."

"Not astrology—" Noah said, instantly knowing it was wrong to do so.

"I know!" Liam snapped, "I know! Not Libra, Scorpio: Astrophysics."

The moment passed in Liam's own patience. There was in his question of a vantage on everything a sense which encompassed the extraordinary (impossible, really) landscape before them on the screen. For a while then their silence seemed to weave in and out of its own canyons. Then slowly, amazingly (too much to hope for between a father and a son on the cusp of something), they began to talk of things that mattered to them, the talk not quite a path but a foothold, each of them pointing some newly seen element or changing ones, each describing the scene they saw, its apprehensions and delights.

The camera floated into a side valley where cramped piñon clung to rocky ledges and tufted hollows with their needles. Noah briefly considered telling Liam about Pete Ehmer and their talks under the pine trees in the summer before college but he was already too much struck with a feeling of melancholy and the void.

"Then why do we live?" Liam had asked, walking helplessly (for Noah at least) into the shadow of his own melancholy.

Noah tried to explain it away at first, trying to explain to Liam how he had thought about something Cathleen shared with him once, a French philosopher, a priest, who talked about how if who we are is present in us from the instant we are born then it is important to ask what constitutes the continuity of the same strand of life shared by both the newly kindled consciousness at someone's birth and the complex consciousness that same person has become later in life.

"Life can't be that, you see," Noah said. "It can't be only a sum of what you saw and were, or else all that came before would not have been life either."

Liam was impatient a little, his impatience less however, Noah thought, with the father than with the logic. In fact the whole conversation was largely without impatience, surprising perhaps for a father and son.

Liam's resistance was itself a refutation of the logic, Noah knew. The problem with the kernel of life argument was how it did not account for the actual portion of the person who Liam, Cathleen or any of the others Noah loved provided him.

Like Liam he felt angry and frustrated that what they were now might not exist after death. The French priest had argued that the same strand remained among the living after death, that we literally kept people alive in memory by denying their death in the way we lived our lives.

This was why Cathleen had shared the reading with him. For her it seemed like what poetry did. That night with Liam, however, it seemed empty to him, only words.

The anger and the frustration and the emptiness had left him feeling sad and when Liam inevitably drifted away to the telephone or video game or whatever called him the feelings eventually drove Noah from their house into the darkened garage and the leather upholstered womb of the Lexus. He hadn't left the garage that night because he knew it wasn't possible to outdistance these feelings in time or space alike, and because, he supposed, he had hoped Cathleen would come out to pluck him from the darkness. Similar feelings likewise left him sad and haunted now, driving out on an absurd errand to see an ancient lady client he hardly knew, his wife and son far from home.

It wasn't a car crash, their conversation, but it was a moment, a moment had come and gone, like television, the spray of light receding to a ghost dot in the darkness and then darkness into darkness gone.

CHAPTER THREE

Butter

The wide wide world lay beneath them, serene from where they clung to butter hill.

The Wide Wide World was the title of the novel written by Miss Susan Warner under the name of Elizabeth Wetherell, its popularity exceeded in its time only by *Uncle Tom's Cabin*. It was a lugubrious book, treacly and dark, yet compelling as an eddy. It kept drawing you out and out on its long sad water.

A girl named Ellen is torn from her dying mother by her brusque and unthinking father and sent off on her own in the wide wide world to live in the country with cruel and distant relatives.

The Misses Warner, Susan and her sister Anna, rowed out on Sundays from Constitution Island to West Point where they conducted religious services and then watched parades and enjoyed picnics at Monument Point with the cadets before rowing home. Before they died, old women near the middle of another century by then, they had sold off most of their possessions and fixtures merely to cling to the island while they hoped to interest the Secretary of War in keeping it unspoiled and public in perpetuity.

The wide wide world was full of sadness.

Constitution Island lay south of here, she had named it for Liam as part of a litany, one of the names recited in a primer of this place: Bull Hill, Breakneck, Cold Spring, Constitution Island. In the canyon of the river below them turkey buzzards circled in slow spirals on the updrafts and lazily drifted up past them and away above the mountain.

They sat in the sunlight on the edge of the most beautiful place in the wide wide world and she was full of sadness. She wondered whether it was only that her son, her only son, was going away and that this ledge would be the last place they would linger in a certain life.

It was possible, even likely, that a feeling like this colored her mood. But she wanted him to grow away, it was what she raised him for, and in fact in some sense she longed to come again and sit here with the man he would become. She thought her sadness was something nearer. He had been afraid on the road over the mountain and his fear hurt and saddened her. Anyone would be afraid there, a two lane strip of asphalt slathered like molasses on an upturned plum pudding.

She hadn't dared to say anything so quaint. Anyone would be afraid and he didn't know it and she couldn't say that either, not then. She had taken a vow of silence and so instead she watched the beads of sweat form on his forehead, his knuckles turn white and quiver on the wheel, and she fought to stay silent through his own raw and ugly litany of fuck and shit and cocksuck and bastard.

When young men, or any, had no words for their fear they used these ones. Still it was ugly and it hurt her; she hated to see him go off wordless.

He hadn't used the one word she reserved as her own, the one she had forbidden him, the one with the thumping sound of a hollow squash or ripe melon. Cunt was a word only a woman could say and then only under the most particular of circumstances.

"You can't forbid him words," Noah had said when she first told him. He had a lawyer's sense of language. Liam was perhaps eight years old then.

"Maybe forbid isn't the right term," she allowed. "Some words are reserved. Cunt and fag come to mind."

And kill and hate and lie she hadn't said.

"He'll use them anyway," Noah said.

"I'm sure he will, without me," she said. "It isn't a rule, it's a melody."

I love my cunt with you she told Noah soon after, certain he would recognize the melody, though then as sometimes she feared he could understand neither word nor thing.

The road over Storm King was a hard one on account of both its beauty and its peril. A driver wanted to look out where the Hudson gaped below, yet traffic kept coming at you and meanwhile the shoulderless road wound relentlessly away. It took two passes to stop at the overlook near the summit: you had to go over the mountain and then back again in order to be heading the right way to attempt to park in the narrow apron where two cars could barely fit bumper to bumper. Often the apron was occupied and you descended into Cornwall and then up and back again if you had the patience. Even when there was space to park, the cars behind you balked at slowing and pure momentum threatened to sweep you past it. No one could

LIAM'S GOING

expect an eighteen year old, even a generally fearless one, to
master such a Zen-like practice of driving easily. No one, that
is, except himself.

"Well fuck that goddamn shit," he fumed and stormed unmindful from the car, nearly clipping off the door of the Volvo
in the process, swinging it open into the narrow traffic they had
just escaped. He vaulted the low stone wall and strode out onto
the rocks as if, a Storm King himself, he had a mind to walk out
into air and across to Mount Taurus.

"I wish we were fucking there already, if we stayed on the
goddamn Thruway we fucking would be. We could have driven
in a day."

She nearly laughed despite the sadness. Fuck that goddamn
shit. Fucking would be. These were such sodden and unmusi-
cal phrases, he really didn't know yet how to curse with any
music. "Holy blue jumping Jesus!" her grandfather used to say.
Still he was handsome in the wind, fuck yes, her son, his blond
hair whipped into angelic broth like Keats' hair, though shorter
as was the fashion again.

It was a would-be Keats who renamed the mountain. N. P.
Willis, Nathaniel Parker, was known even in his own time as
"the dude poet of the Hudson." He was more subdivision de-
veloper than poet, the kind of person who plats roads from a
seed catalogue into Daphne Lane and Hibiscus Circle. A front
man and self-appointed flack for the Hudson River romantics,
he was nonetheless said by contemporary accounts to be curly
haired and pink-cheeked like Liam. At least one thing she had
read about him suggested he had an eye for life whether he generally exercised it or not. On a certain occasion, tired of the pale

gentry about him, he went out on the lower turnpike through the Irish settlements where the gentry never traveled. He looked upon the Irish like wildflowers and reported finding "a certain relief in a mile or two of jolly and careless faces" outside the colorless cultivation.

Once her own dude poet stopped storming they sat and let the sadness settle into silence for a time, watching buzzards rise and a blue barge plow up the river before its red tug. She had an absurd attack of nostalgia. There was a book about a tugboat she used to read to Liam when he was a small boy, a book of his father's, a tugboat named Mike as best she could remember. To ward off foolish melancholy she recited the names of the places below them, first south toward West Point, then north past Polopel's Island to Plum Point and the Newburgh bridge.

A boy still, like any boy he was caught by the ruined turrets of the island. She told him the story of the Bannerman castle and how the secondhand munitions dealer stored his excess weapons and powder there until they blew away his pre-Disney fantasy in the nineteen twenties, leaving this ruin to mark his folly.

"How foolish we men are," he said deadpan. He was coming around.

"And don't you forget it," she said and hugged him and he let her.

"I'm sorry you are stuck with me," she said. "I just don't like to drive as much as you and your father do."

Stuck with me was wrong, she meant she was sorry the trip was so long. For anyone else it really would have been a day.

Liam ignored her apology. She let him go.

"How do you know all this stuff?" he asked, making a sweeping gesture to take in the river.

"I read a great deal back then. I loved this river."

And had a lover here once in these hills.

"How do you still know so much now?"

"I see it in the hills. It's like reading them. Like memory."

"What good does it do?" he asked. "I mean remembering all these things."

The question was like a slap to her, but when she looked at him he was blank faced, curled up within himself in the way he did these past few years. She had imagined he might be searching the hills and the river trying to see what she read there. Instead he was looking elsewhere.

"Well?" he asked. Now he looked at her.

She realized she had not answered his question.

What good does it do, she wondered.

"It doesn't do good," she said. "It is good. Memory is what goodness is."

"That's easy for you to say," he said. It wasn't a challenge, his tone more wistful than challenging.

He smiled sheepishly, winning her back.

"Did you ever write about it?" he asked.

"No."

He didn't question this and it was a relief to her. The river and its history for her were things she kept as her own, not disowned but over. It was not long after she learned this river that she left it and went home to her husband where they set off to bring about Liam's birth. Yet she could not help but wonder now whether not writing about this valley formed the unmarked sign, the fold, the scarlet letter in disappearing ink. Could it be that our sins are perhaps under erasure as the postmodernists say, but like a secret penned in lemon juice they reappear in the sunlight.

What sins, she wondered. Was solitary love a sin?

She wondered at how she stirred now at the word, even the memory of sin. A longing rose in her dimly like the feeling of ovulation, signaling a cyclic turn deep within. What would she give birth to now with her only son gone, her womb and words alike long dried into some approximation of ripeness. For an instant she was as afraid as he had been on the thin road up here. Then she turned back to the river, the continuing story.

"It's been the same through the ages," she said. "The marshes around Constitution Island were polluted with cadmium from a battery factory the army built after the second world war. The roots of the reeds are polluted still and any fish or bird that bottom feeds or eats these plants either dies or turns monstrous. They fester and grow extra limbs."

Jesus, she thought, listen to me! How a small penance turns Cathleen to Cassandra. A womb filled with toads and monsters.

She told him a happier story hoping to change their luck. It was nearly time to go, she could see him fret and rock upon the boulder where they sat. He was eager to be there, in the future. Yet the Hudson was green as stone and the blue sky was feathered with white and for a while she would claim her indulgence as poet and mother.

"There is a story told about a young minister who loved a girl who lived near here. She was also loved by a farm boy who of course didn't stand a chance to win her hand from someone fine."

She watched his eyes for signs of the turning inward. She watched for boredom or annoyance. She tested his heart in this and she knew it wasn't fair, though still she did so like the mother in a story testing the young suitor of her daughter.

"Well, one winter evening the minister took the young girl out on the ice of the river for a sleigh ride, courting her. As they neared the island there—"

She paused here and risked a gesture and his eyes followed out across the water below and her heart leapt as it had in other years reading to him about Tugboat Mike or Catherine ni Houlihan.

"—the ice broke and the sleigh went in and the minister clung to the jagged ice unable to save her or him."

She watched his eyes squint and she thought she saw them moisten.

"It happened that the farm boy was nearby and he rushed to their rescue, pulling them each up onto the ice and, after covering them with his own blankets, even leading the horse to shore. When the minister saw how his beloved clung to the farm boy, he knew she loved the boy in a way she never could love him."

She had lost heart toward the end of the story but pushed on for Liam's sake as much as hers. She didn't want to embarrass him on account of his attention to her.

"The minister blessed them both," she said, "and promised to prevail with her father and then preside at their wedding."

Prevail was the wrong word she knew. What had she meant? It was the suitor who prevailed not the interlocutor.

In the real world of course love didn't win out as easily. Powers prevailed, ranks of angels, dominions. Ministers read providence in rescue. It didn't do to fill a young man's heart with stories of love triumphant, even true stories.

In the real world, she thought darkly, it was just as likely that piety and power might drown before the dull witness and avenging eyes of boys without words to say what they were doing or allowing to be done. Pale fingers slipping from the jagged edges of paler ice.

She knew nothing of the real world and briefly (briefly) wanted to cast herself over this cliff, to fly away before he left her, before the pain began.

His or hers, love lost or gained.

Liam studied the distance where motor boats plied the water in white strings of soundless wake. A freight train passed on the tracks across the flats below, its noises rising.

"How would you feel if Dad had an affair with someone?" he asked.

The question stunned her. It pinned her down and drained any thought of casting off. What did he know of either of them.

"Why?" she asked. "Is he?"

It felt ugly to ask, worse when he reddened and sputtered.

"My god, no!" he said, "I mean not that I know. Oh jesus damn, that's worse. It was dumb, I'm sorry. I was just thinking of your story and what you asked me about being true to Jennie."

He was nearly crying. She took his hand and laughed.

"No, I'm the one who should be sorry," she said. "It was a foolish thing to ask. If Noah had an affair, I would know. I would. It was a reflex reaction, not just an unfair but an unnecessary thing to ask you."

She kissed the hand and gave it back to him. There were

other people there on this overlook, a dark couple speaking Arabic, their plump son in dress shorts and knee socks and perforated sandals, his hair black and as tightly curled as Esau's.

"I'd feel hurt of course," she said, "but I would love him. I do. I have and will, whatever happens."

"It wasn't what I meant to ask," he said. "It just came out, like your question. I was thinking all sorts of things while you told the story."

"What sorts?" she asked. "Should we finish this in the car?"

He shook his head. No, the car and college would wait a moment more.

"What do you suppose happens when we die?" he asked.

My god, she thought, sometimes it all comes out in a blurt for a young man. This made them easy to love. There had been times when they would talk like this, mother and son, but they hadn't done so for a time and the ones before had mostly surprised her by slipping up out of the routine. This one came in drama and expanse, it was unexpected. He rather than her had cast himself off a cliff.

"When we die?" she asked. "Or after?"

"After," he said. "When is too hard to think about."

He wants to know about death. She wants to know about love. It is a test of ages. Her love was true like an arrow is true, direct. She loved her husband and her son and language and the wide wide world. The only question was did she love them well enough, could one love another well enough to ward off what was too hard to think about, or better still to think well enough about it.

"I think we live," she said. "In a place like this I cannot help but think we live. There are spirits everywhere in these mountains."

She turned to ask him what he thought and his eyes were red and his lip had pale indentations where he had bit it. She suspected he had been crying and had wiped the tears away before she could see them.

There was no way to ask.

"Should we go?" she said. "I think we're each a little loco from the heights and worried about what we have ahead."

She offered him the car keys again but he shook them off in silence and then perversely crawled into the back seat, wedging himself in with the boxes and electronic gear as if trying to disappear entirely.

She got behind the wheel and on the way back down the mountain going the wrong way toward Cornwall still wanting to tell him the story of the dude poet and how he changed the name of Butter Hill to Storm King. After making the requisite U-turn in the parking lot of a nature preserve to get themselves heading back up Storm King in the right direction, they headed once more up and over and, she knew, away not just from childhood and the past but from the possibility of ever again telling certain kinds of stories in the same way.

Liam was talking to himself, or so she thought. She tried to see what he was doing back there but he had slouched down like a tank commander below where she could see easily in the mirror. She turned her head just a second to glance back at him and in the process swerved slightly into the other lane where a van blared its horn.

"Fucking shit!" Liam shouted, cupping Noah's cell phone in his hand.

She cut the wheel harder than was necessary.

He had been talking to someone, most likely Jennie, although she supposed it could be his father as well. There was no way of knowing.

In the instant between the veering and the blare she had met his eyes and found in them a stranger.

Something was undone. She tried to find him in the mirror again. The episode had brought him back into view, upright and vigilant as if intent upon keeping her from almost killing them again.

He didn't seem to see that she was still shaking from the scare.

He went on talking a while on the phone in a low whisper and then hung up, retreating into his earphones again, staring blankly out the window at the passing scene.

They had briefly come so close on the edge of the mountain, she thought, thinking not of the veering but the conversation before it and his solemn question.

Now he slouched there like a stranger.

What happens when we die?

How much could fit in a moment?

It was funny in a way, what had happened. At first she had thought he was mumbling to her from the seat. Then she was sure he was talking aloud to himself. Then, weirdly, she imagined he might be recording some recollection of this moment, a play-by-play version of oral history, into the little voice-activated tape recorder Noah had given him.

She remembered this sequence clearly. My life is flashing before my eyes, she thought. She wanted to recount it to him, to explain her veering, but the blank eyes warded her off.

There was so much more she longed to tell him. Of John Keats' curls and the story of the Christmas Eve when he discovered negative capability. Of how quickly a life passes and a child grows old. Of the nature of love and how what we look back from beckons.

She lay in the arms of her lover only twice and never on a feather bed or any for that matter. Once in an apple barn and a last time in a forgotten graveyard. O what happens when we die, she thought, what happens ever after.

Between times there was laughter and apples and trips along the river. Even some Italian. It turned out that Paul loved Dante and she loved this in him and loving things about him made the summer away from Noah go faster, as fast as a carousel sometimes.

It took time to learn this, however. First they began to parse the word passion and she learned to love *truit au bleu*.

"What happened to your happy marriage?" Paul had asked her.

This was before they were lovers, the afternoon she asked him if he wanted to have dinner with her. It was one of the signs of his grace that he never said something as awkward as this once they were lovers.

"It's happier than ever," she said. "I feel strong enough to be friends with you, despite whatever attraction."

"It's a strange friendship that means to spite attraction," he said.

They stood in the sunshine near the fruit stand. She had purchased berries from him, a square wooden basket of plump blueberries which stained the wood in plum circles.

She smiled. "You are right, of course," she said. "Not despite passion, but informed by it."

She had amplified the tenor of the term, she knew, from attraction to passion. They each let it pass. Yet it rose within her, giddy, nameless, attraction, passion, whatever.

"*Parleremo Italiano?*" he asked. "Will we talk Italian?"

"God I hope not," she said, "I haven't learned the future tense."

She knew it was a laden phrase, even then. "Let's talk apples," she said.

Qualunque còsa, she thought, the words coming in an instant: whatever.

"*Certo,*" he said. "We won't even eat Italian, we'll have French."

He knew a place with *truit au bleu*. It was off in the hills south somewhere. She was nervous as a bride dressing for the dinner and worried that she worried over what underwear to wear. She wore thick brown sandals and a long brown linen dress over satin, the brown she knew setting off her tan to advantage.

She had called Noah to say she was having dinner with a friend.

"In case you were going to call," she said, "I mean I didn't want you to worry."

He wasn't worried, he was distracted. He had taken the opportunity of her absence to overwork. In those days it was something he would have done daily without her, and nonetheless still did so often she had sometimes to recall him to what they had together. He was hungry for success and he loved to lawyer in a way few men do.

"I'm glad you are making friends at school," he said. It was something of a teasing remark but he meant it. She wondered whether she should correct the misapprehension. She considered briefly a reply in kind: We share the same play group. He pushes me on the swing.

"I love you so," she said, foolish tears in her eyes and voice.

"O I know you do Katie," he said, he alone ever on earth using this name.

They hung up and she realized he hadn't asked if the friend was a man or a woman. She knew it really wouldn't matter to him.

"Ah Heloise," Paul said when she met him. She had driven past the fruit stand and up along the dirt road to the farm and parked the car in front of his dark green nineteen fifty-four Chevrolet pickup truck. Further back under the shade of the black walnut trees there was a rusty Volvo.

"I'm sorry," she said. She didn't get the reference at first. She was thinking of the woman who wrote hints for housewives in the newspapers.

"Your garb," he said, "is nunly. Brown dress, brown sandals. Heloise and Abelard."

"He was castrated by her family," she said calmly. "All that came after. Is the Volvo yours as well?"

He nodded.

"Black hole," she said. "When two of them collide."

"Now there's a start," he said. "Shall we try again?"

"Hello," he said, "I'm happy you are here. Would you like to tour the orchard and the barns before we go?"

She laughed. "Maybe another time," she said. It was a truce and a commonplace and it drained the tension.

"I would like you to meet my mother," he said.

How he said it made her almost dizzy (even in recollection).

He meant these words exactly: it was he who truly wanted the her she was to meet the woman his mother was.

Inside the brick Victorian house it was cooler even than the shade of the black walnut, cooler than the twilight exhalation of the orchard. The house smelled of lavender and something faintly powdery and fleshed. They walked over wide plank floors covered with rag rugs. Inside the house was neither a valentine nor a faded book of fabric swatches. Instead it had the spare quality of bones, lots of light even at evening, Shaker wood rather than upholstery in most places. There was no music, no sound really except the birds outside settling into the trees.

"Mother?" he called out when they had navigated a central hall to a dimmer space at the rear of the house.

The woman who strode out displayed none of the frailness Cathleen had allowed herself to imagine. She was clearly old but rosy, not spry but kinetic, thin in a full denim skirt but radiant-eyed and welcoming. Eyes were her feature, like her son, insistent eyes like tropical fish.

"Mother, this is my friend, Cathleen. She came to us through the fruit stand. My mother, Evelyn," he said.

Evelyn shook her hand and pressed it with her other.

"There's almost nothing there as yet," Evelyn said. "Just wait until our apples!"

She meant the fruit stand: what drew her to them. The voice was frailer than the person yet it sang a little with a sense of laughter under.

"Cathleen is a poet," Paul said to the one. "Mother is eighty," he said to the other.

"He thinks these things in balance," his mother said, this time the laughter present not under. "There's a certain poetry in aging."

"Jesus," Paul said, "I've had an awful start all around tonight."

"Woman twist his tongue," his mother said. "Watch out."

"Cathleen is very married," Paul said. "She's a friend. She loves the valley. I'm showing her around and telling her stories."

"Watch out more so!" his mother said. Both she and Cathleen laughed.

Paul was flustered yet he looked on his mother warmly as he explained himself to Cathleen, "I only meant to say that I am the result of a late and enduring passion. My mother had a family of daughters before me. The two countesses live in California and Baden Baden."

"Stop that! you acerbic boy," his mother said, still laughing. "You'll lose what you gained with your smart tongue." She turned to Cathleen. "That 'late and enduring passion' was a nice touch, I'd say, wouldn't you Cathleen?"

"Yes," she said. This day they were parsing passion.

"Alright, done! Off!" Evelyn became the matriarch, swooshing them off with a smile and the offer of an ivory hand. "Welcome to our house, Cathleen. Please come back again. I would enjoy hearing your poetry."

Outside she asked him. "Countesses?"

"They lead busy lives. They regularly send mother cards and they alternate semiannual visits. I am officially bitter about them. I am not sure whether mother did as well raising daughters."

It was such a sweet thing to say. Evelyn had raised him well.

For a moment she had not wanted to drive away. It might have been a passionate foreboding a foreboding about passion but even then she thought it was as much that she simply wished to stay and hear from this lively woman about raising daughters and a son as she and Noah were about to do.

Instead, Cathleen strode purposely to the green pickup truck. There might have been a question about the cars but she removed it in movement, named it afterward. Like passion.

"It's like riding an egg," she said as he trundled the truck down the lane to the road, shifting through the gears with an impossibly long gear shift which looked like a black walking stick.

"A life lived in comparison," he said. He was reassuming the laconic self lost briefly in the successive episodes of awkwardness and sweetness. "It's a surprisingly ruddy little truck," he said.

She wondered if he meant rugged. He thought she meant that the truck was fragile as an egg.

"I was talking about the way the cab curves," she said, "like an egg."

Also like the hills. They made their way by back roads to the Taconic and then down through the moonrise into the hills south and east of Poughkeepsie. They kept the windows rolled down for the coolness and so talked very little. The restaurant was stone bistro with a trout pool, Japanese lanterns, and roses on dark blue trellises. The proprietor, a stocky and elegant man with razor cut gray-hair, looking something like Matisse. "Ah Monsieur Paul," he said. "Madame," he said and bowed. Inside the bistro was cool as a well.

To be known, she thought, was very romantic. The night was a fairyland and, in fact, by its end she felt known in some new sense. It was very heady, very full of laughter. Paul told stories of the countesses and the Italian tree men, of his old loves and the comparative costs of wood and cardboard apple bushels. She

MICHAEL JOYCE

told the story of Noah's benchmade shoes and the dill bread
and how much they loved each other. The best of his stories
about old loves involved a woman named Alearda, a painter
and wood sprite who lived alone in a cabin along the Hudson
beyond the railway tracks near Rhinecliff and whom he wooed
in Italian and pidgen and flute music and apple blossoms but
who went home nonetheless to the small town of San Costanzo
in the Marche where she lived in a tower vined with caper bushes
and sometimes sent notes which smelled of lavender.

Over coffee Paul begged a poem and Cathleen recited the
short one which began with the spider's thread caught in sunlight. It wasn't her best poem in any sense, but he saw the image.

"I know what you mean, how they gleam in the light an
instant and then you can't see them and so you wonder if the
world is strung with unnoticed silk," he said.

In her delight at this recognition she realized she had been
testing him. Unnoticed silk was a lovely phrase, his not hers,
and it stirred her.

She, for her part, had failed an earlier test, although it wasn't
one he posed to her rather one she imposed upon herself.
Though fairly finished, first by a girlhood and an adolescence
of hungry reading and then by Oberlin and its insistences and
finally by what began to be a poet's life and her situation, if not
her role as an esquire's wife, she nonetheless knew there were
occasional rough spots. To Cathleen these were burrs of the
sort her father would grind from things at his workbench in a
roostertail of sparks. Normally she prided herself in not knowing certain details withheld from persons of her social class, the
use of the serrated spoon crosswise at the top of the formal

~86~

place setting, the desperately quaint "elevensies." She was twenty-seven years old, sure of herself, and a little angry about something that had to do with her condition.

Even so she was mistaken about the nature of *truit au bleu* which she somehow had convinced herself (a girlhood spent in reading) involved the death by boiling of live trout. It seemed unnecessarily cruel to her, an epicurean obscenity. In her mind it was not far from the spectacle of Japanese businessmen eating live lobster sushi which she had seen on television, the seagreen creatures thrashing across the table with the transparent flesh of their tails exposed.

"My god, who could blame you," Paul said when she fervently explained all this.

"Though I'm afraid this is one of those dishes about the moment. And simplicity. The poor things are dispatched in an instant, gutted and then plunged, albeit before they have stopped twitching."

"They are dead?" she asked.

"Well, who can say what constitutes the death of any creature," he attempted a smile. "They are dead when they come out of the water," he said, "and sweet as air. It's his specialty but we can each have something other if it alarms you."

"No, no," she said and felt wanting. Why? She had wondered about this moment through the years in the way scruples haunt you, had even written a poem about trout after Noah took up fly fishing. One verse described the *bleu*. The poem was of course influenced by Schubert and was often anthologized. It was good, she thought, to commemorate the secret foolishness of your youth and she wished as much for her son.

Still the poem avoided the truth she knew, despite her, how the blue trout had stood for something alien and sinful she wished nonetheless to know. In some part of her she still did, even now.

After they were back on the road a while Liam stripped off the earphones and sat up again and she mistook it for an opening.

"Do you remember those worlds you made?" she asked him. "Your adventures? All those notebook pages of rivers and mountains and tunnels and whatnot?"

"Of course I do," he said, a little uneasily. She should have left it there.

"Do you ever look at them and wonder what they meant?"

"Meant?" he said. There was an increasing edge in his voice. Even without the near mishaps on the mountain it was too much to think a two-day car trip would not have its irritations. "I looked at a bunch of the notebooks just yesterday or sometime whatever day it was! while I was packing. I have them all."

Not all, she thought. Sometimes a mother takes the best worlds for her own. She had saved two or three of the most ornate maps, the ones tinted with thin crayon, limned with markers, walls of carefully cobbled pen strokes, forests of spines.

"They don't *mean* anything," he said. "They just are."

"A poet said that once about poetry," she said.

"I'm not an idiot," he said. "We did have poetry courses."

"You are tired and snappish and ungracious," she said, herself peeved, then took a breath. "I'm sorry," she said, "I pushed it."

"I'm sorry too," he said, unsorry, and submerged again into the noise of the earphones.

She was wrong, she knew, but he was wrong to push her away. He learned this from his father, untaught but tutored nonetheless, they each held their worlds within and, when she wished to glimpse, offered her the black hole. Not the black hole of two solid cars colliding but the negative of energy, everything that poetry was not.

Unpoem of no thingness.

Wordplay.

"I, too, dislike it," she recited Marianne Moore about poetry, sounding the lines into the automobile silence. "There are things more important beyond this fiddle." Liam squirreled his nose and looked blankly through the side window. She loved him in profile, he would steal the hearts of women. Fuck him.

The appearance of this imprecation shocked her. She wondered what or whom was she cursing. Did she damn him for her love of him or damn those whose love would eventually, and naturally, take him away from her? Or was she merely taking up his language against him?

Well then damn him anyway and damn all remnants and leavings.

Where was the "place for the genuine" that Moore had consoled herself with in the poem? Late in her life Moore had revised her poem that contained this argument and clipped it there, at the genuine, as if all she had written after it was boodle.

Even as she fumed or was it him who did? she genuinely loved her boy, her would-be, already almost was, sometimes man. She loved him in profile or straightaway or as he receded into distance, broad back and valiant hair to her.

Still sometimes he peeved her. If the truth be told the notebook adventures had peeved her terribly. For years in every car ride she would be tied to him by time and space and his father's inattention, torn from the books she meant to read, the poems to write, the reveries and memories and mindless nothingnesses, taken instead through these endless chronicles of what never was.

"Look, here's the Castle and there are two dragons that can't die and one has huge teeth and you fall through his throat into the lagoon and then there are three armies of Mardor."

Murder? No some made-up name or worse a name from a faux-Tolkien television version of adolescent fantasy.

He would scrawl these maps for hours and then recite their topographies and mythologies and armories and then insist you play the game which always involved an endless set of choices followed by gaps and slippages between page and page of still more maps and choices. He could become a monster of singleness with these tales and so she evolved a way to answer him as if she were auditing while she tried in vain to dream or at least attend to the endless elsewhere outside the car windows.

Sometimes he would catch her. "Why did you say 'yes'? I didn't ask you anything. Are you listening?"

Other times he actually tested her. "Who are the Orc Firelings?"

"I know who they are. You told me before. In that other world."

"Which one?"

"I don't have to be grilled like this, you know," she would say, "I am paying attention and I don't have to prove that to you."

In the game, too, he would ask her question after question, mapping her progress through each page with a squiggle from his pen, writing over all he had labored to prepare (and never using a pencil to mark this progress, despite her urging). In between the questions, which were nothing more than the commonplace decisions of computer games, there would be stretches of exposition within which he seemed to recall the construction of the space. She longed for these patches, they were clearings in a thicket. She could lose her mind a bit while he told the stories to her because they were really stories he told himself.

What were they, she wondered now, what satisfactions, what symmetries? Despite his best efforts, even at the times she summoned some excitement or interest or the occasional times when his father played and she drove (Noah being more suited to the choice of knife or spear—she would exasperate her son by refusing to fight a monster: "You'll die!" he'd threaten. "If I die, I die," she would say. "It will be awful," he would say, "they tear your eyes out and burn you with starfire." "So be it," she would say, the picture of peace, more fervid than either son or father in this insistence), the games always seemed to end in a sense of emptiness and impotence.

There was no outcome and yet he longed for thrall and satisfaction.

Perhaps that was what the game was about, she thought now, understanding that the unfolding really is all, that we make our thralls only after.

Noah thought it was simple. "The games are about sex," he said. "The insides of women. He goes from page to page by stroking them with his pen. There are all these mysterious orifices and outcropping. The castles have nipples."

"Thank you counselor Freud," she said. "Why don't you take

him down to the whorehouse like grandpa used to do and we'll be done with all the damned notebooks."

It hurt Noah when she treated him as if he didn't know anything, as if he were a man. Life raising a son tested their simplicity and their sense of who they each were. That was its purpose, its meaning, its thrall.

Noah was probably right. The force of the maps and the game was a thrust into the complexity, into the interconnectedness of things, like the invisible and silken threads of spiders. There were times, not many although increasing as he aged, when Liam would play the games entirely alone. Toward the end the stories he told in the clearings had their own fascinations and sometimes held her in their poetry.

"Where did you come up with that phrase?" she would ask. "Is that from you or from TV?"

"Me," he'd say, "or TV," it didn't matter to him, he found his fascinations both without and within.

He was right about this, of course, but as wrong as the poet had been about what things mean. Even what only "is" must mean, she thought, or what sense of us.

The isness means in unwindings. We are our complications. Everything that was, is.

Jesus, she knew nothing.

Perhaps that was what had assailed her about these games, how they brought her face to face with the nothingness of language. Sometimes her own poems even seemed like the skeletons of birds, memories of flight, chalky bones, mere patterns. It was all a word game, masturbating with words but without the spew boys enjoyed, or so she imagined not knowing what boys enjoyed or, for that matter, men either, at least of the spew.

What she did know was that nonetheless or perhaps because of these games before long Liam became a wonderful writer.

He slept now inside a world of noise, almost post-coitally, surrounded by his meager possessions, exhausted by all he wanted. Still no thrall. No spew.

In the days before they left home Liam had slept with Jennie under their roof. Cathleen had never imagined that life could come to this, not that she was a prude nor naive about his generation and friends. They talked of everything; she knew when he and Jennie first made love. It was just the commonplace of it which she resisted.

"I can't allow it, I'm sorry," she said. "I feel responsible for Jennie."

"I've slept with her in her house," he said. "You can call her mother."

"Jesus," she said. "I won't. No. Have her call me."

She could not contemplate the call. Shall we discuss my son's wand of flesh within your daughter, her plump breasts upon his hairless chest?

Noah didn't know what to say. "Actually there's no real liability since sexual majority in this state comes before legal majority. Unless, of course, she gets pregnant."

He wasn't joking. She wished he were.

"Did you just say what you just said?" she asked him, aghast. "Is that the best you can do."

She realized now that they were all more stressed than they were able to admit. Having Jennie sleep over was a feint, a fumbling kind of recognition.

It was, finally, just that, a sleep-over, almost comic. Jennie's mother called and earnestly explained her morality until Cathleen asked her the question about whether she could ever have imagined her life coming to this and they both laughed. "I'm just not comfortable," Cathleen said.

"Well, then, you shouldn't do it," Jennie's mother said.

"Christ," Cathleen said, "we're replaying the conversations I had with my girlfriends in high school about 'doing it'!"

They laughed again. "I'll think about it," she said. Jennie came over that night with a knapsack for an overnight bag. They rented a movie—nothing terribly romantic, an early Truffaut film actually and Cathleen and Noah watched it with them. Jennie and Liam made butter popcorn. After the movie they said goodnight and went to bed.

"I should have given her towels. Now it's too late," Cathleen said. "Should we fuck too?" she asked Noah, "set the whole house banging like shutters in the wind?"

They were neither of them certain they could manage it under the circumstances. They watched some more television. Cathleen piled extra towels in the bathroom. The house was silent. They managed it. In the morning Cathleen made pancakes and wept for no reason.

She was surprised at what she would have done that night in the darkness and perfume of the apple barn. Despite the warmth she felt within, despite the burning, she began to shake with a chill that would not go away and drove home through the moonlight with the heater on in the Volvo. She didn't see Paul for weeks.

In the interim she learned some Italian and more still about the mid-Hudson valley.

"*I casi della vita sono tanti,*" she copied the beginning of a story into her notebook and her memory. The simple phrase seemed infinitely heart-breaking.

—As life holds so many possibilities.

It was a rascal tale, with a twist, chosen because the language was simple enough for beginners. Not Dante but Montale. To each her paradise.

"*E trovandomi una sera in trattoria con Stephani.*"

—And I found myself in a restaurant with Stephen.

"*Trovandomi*" is our state, she had thought even then. Finding ourselves in once upon a time. Trovandomi, the word even sounded like a shake of the dice, the future rolling out with the click of bones.

"*Così, tra un discorso e i'altro, gli domandai se si sentiva capace di scrivermi una lettura.*"

—I asked him in the midst of talking about one thing or another, whether he was capable of writing me a letter.

This too she knew, the poet's situation, likewise *trovandomi*. Finding oneself called out by a story in the midst of talk about one thing or another.

"*Come di uno che abbia fame, sia disoccupato, abbia a carico la madre malata di un male che non perdona e.*"

—As though it were written by someone hungry, out of work, and burdened with the support of a mother struck by a fatal disease.

She remembered laughing aloud at this turn, for the first time feeling something really Italian in Italian. The turn from our

MICHAEL JOYCE

fortune to fraud, *"come di uno,"* just like someone. Like anyone. All life eventually ending that way anyway thankless, helpless, hungry, mother dead or dying, you following after why not make a killing on it now? The name of the story was "La Parola Mamma," the word mother, and the rascal is eventually done in by the writer who sells the same letter to another. This, too, an old story, not Dante but Lennon and McCartney, the paperback writer who could change styles every week or two.

She changed round the way she moved through the valley for a while as well. Life then was so simply linked, she thought, as if a word game or one of Liam's adventures. All life eventually connecting that way anyway theatrical, haphazard, happenchance, youth passed or passing why not enjoy it while it lasts? She couldn't. It wasn't that easy for her.

She found a different way out of Rhinecliff, not back past Paul's fruit stand but south along the thin lavender light of the river seen gaping through the trees beyond the cliffs, continuing on past a mansion or two set off by meadows and eventually down to the Mill Road and the pond not far from Staatsburg which she already knew. There were other fruit stands, though none as sweet. She thought as much then in romantic confusion and even now in retrospect.

Even so life holds so many possibilities. There was often in those weeks at dusk a blue heron on the mill pond, regal, silent, dull, somehow tragic, too nervous for its visage or the width of its wings, apt to quick flight a circle of the dimming pond, sometimes resettling at the far end, sometimes away into failing light yet finally stolid, loyal, constant.

She became (*trovandomi*) a thesaurus of sensibilities.

Could you seduce yourself with your own resistance? she asked herself then.

Of course you can, poor dear, she answered herself a full twenty years after on another shore of the same river. No better way else. We seduce ourselves in what we resist giving over to it, as if we had been taken in the way we once imagined that word would function.

There was a poem she had left behind before she set off with Liam, not a poem but the beginning of one, which she realized now, whether by prescience or accident, had the image of apples beyond reach.

She wished she had it with her, actually or fully in memory. She tried to recall the lines about long love and lasting. Tricky almost metaphysical lines but not, she hoped, tricked up.

Who she was then seemed so young to her, twenty years after, a son at least figuratively by her side. And yet who she was now seemed so emotionally glib and settled to her in comparison to the girl who charted (*come di uno*) every emotion and all the words she knew for them, struggling every instant to know, to know, to know her inner heart and the workings of an uncertain world.

That much she recalled from the draft of the poem on her desk: "what we look back upon/ beckons our understanding."

She had presented herself at Paul's fruit stand at dusk after two weeks.

"Don't you dare say 'long time, no see'," she said.

"My lips are sealed," he said, pressing a forefinger to them.

"Would you like to see something?" she asked.

He mumbled, impish, through the sealed lips and made her laugh.

"You can talk," she said. "Even a princess kisses a frog."

In the mention of a kiss her curious locution was a somewhat daring how-do-you-do, but the phrase "even a princess" presented a curious inversion. Some time afterward he asked her what she meant by it.

"I was confused by excessive logic," she said. "Too muddled at that moment for either passion or poetry."

She succumbed to a mathematics more than a logic and seduced herself in her calculations.

The question at hand had begun for her as one regarding whether happiness proves an impediment itself to free action. She meant that Paul's insistence on her (much vocalized) claim of happiness seemed itself to constrain her. It was as if, respecting her wishes, he (and not just he, she or whoever else, now or ever) suggested that she could not in fact act otherwise.

This, of course, had the effect of making what she chose (Noah in this instance) not a choice but simply an outcome of something prior and—what was worse then, worse still now — invariable.

Also she knew now what she must have been surely was horny. Though that wouldn't have been a word she used then, or should now she supposed except for its shock and the claim it makes on another diction. Her whole self hungered for feeling back then. She hungered still.

Fuck him. Fucked by him, she thought now.

Though that didn't discount all her mathematics, then or now.

Cathleen Hogan's mother Agnes Hogan was a simple and substantial woman, a Catholic, the mother of sons and daughters, a doctor and a poet, a dead soldier, a lapsed priest, one unmarried son (not the priest), one daughter an earnest mother of a similarly large brood as her mother's, and another, the afore-mentioned poet, the mother of one mysterious dark boy, now a young man, Liam. All her life Cathleen Hogan's mother's favorite song was "The Tennessee Waltz" and now (in reverie, she's driving the car and watching her only son) her daughter wonders what romance it meant for someone who grew up a plain girl with plain passions. "He was dancing with my darling and while they were dancing, my friend stole my sweetheart from me," the song went. Cathleen thinks of the picture of her mother, slightly overweight, teenage mother in saddle shoes and lipstick and velvet purse and dreams so clear that they shone through the picture like the aura of sunset. After a certain point her mother had loved no one but her father. (As far as she knew? Cathleen asks herself. No. She knew.) What was it Agnes Hogan saw there in that song? Possibilities? Passions? Or merely the lingering adolescent sweetness of the tragic? A French woman novelist had written a whole erotic novel about someone similarly stolen from a dance. The woman in the photograph, the girl Agnes, had "best chums" who were other girls, had worked in a department store selling perfume, had once swooned over Frank Sinatra, saved a box of excruciatingly beautiful love letters from her husband and augmented the collection every birthday, Christmas, Valentine's, and anniversary with another Cathleen's toolmaker father wrote out with a surprisingly flowing hand in blue ink with an old Waterman fountain pen. Still the Tennessee Waltz could bring tears to Agnes' eyes, tears he was helpless to soothe, tears they all were helpless before.

She thinks about Liam's adventure stories, mere frames for unimagined passions.

She took Paul to see the heron at the mill pond.

"What took you away?" he asked.

She was pleased that he had not said "what kept you away."

She hushed him lest he put the heron to flight before he had a chance to see it. All my passions, she would have said, and the sound of bees took me away.

Instead she took his hand and raised it up before them as a pointer sighting where the heron stood in shadows and cricket-song. Paul hummed in appreciation and kept her hand and she let him do so.

"I want to hear the bees," she whispered.

"It may be too late," he whispered back, then added. "The moon has left the window, you know."

"I know," she said aloud. The heron did not stir. She released Paul's hand. She realized it was she who held him and not he who kept her hand.

On the night of the blue trout they had returned to his house and her car and the wash of the now-high moon. It was fully night, after wine, and there was the question of good-byes.

"Don't go yet," he said, solving it simply enough. "I want to show you something."

"It is late," she had said, mathematical, resisting, but he walked on toward the three-story barn.

Paradise is the scent of a century of apples suffusing barn wood wormed through and kept ever moist with the sweet settling ripeness of the passing seasons. Paul was wise enough to know not to say anything, neither that first night or the one after.

Cathleen found that she could not say anything.

"I never..." she said and what she meant was complicated.

The apple barn was so clearly what it was there was no mystery. Slatted bins to hold the fruit against the ribs of the barn like an arrested rock slide, nearly all empty now except for some few left of last year's crop. The suffusion of the apple perfume precisely itself and really not at all mysterious once the senses said, yes, of course, this is what it would be after so much time. Yet with it came a memory of enchantment that embarrassed her in its naivete and a half-formed and unrequited longing. She recalled being a girl in a department store holding hands with her mother and moving through the cosmetics section on the ground floor. The store was Adam, Meldrum and Anderson. She recalled the three names as if they were the phases of the moon, recalled also the priestesses in white smocks and perfect coal black hair, their lips etched in magenta, the fragrances both beautiful and oppressive. Her mother held her hand firmly but said nothing. This was not a place for them her purposeful footsteps said. But then it happened. An angel. An Italian. A fragrant girl with a sky blue robe wrapped at her waist stood directly in the aisle along their path and mouthed a phrase so magical it threatened to stay with her forever.

"*Che bella ragazza!*" the woman said and blessed her with unction, a swipe at the ear and a touch of the hand, a cream with the fragrance of angels.

"What is it, Mamma?" Cathleen had asked after they had cleared the cosmetics section and come into the steadier fragrance of cotton and leather.

Her mother fished in her purse for a kleenex. In the cosmetics section, she had thanked the girl twice, one in English and once, miraculously, in Italian.

Grazie. Perfectly.

There were mysteries. She declined her mother's ministrations with the kleenex, instead rubbed the cream carefully into her palms.

"You would," her mother had said, smiling, "I should have known you would."

Would. What.

Her mother had never spoken the word fuck, may not have heard it ever. *Grazie.*

She and Paul were in the barn again, on the night of the blue heron, a week or so after the night of the blue trout. They kept time in blue.

"Like many majestic birds," Paul said, "their nests are filthy. All muck and sticks and feathers."

"Like the lotus." Cathleen said.

"Exactly."

There were no bees nor was the moon in the window. On the night of the blue trout Paul had told her how sometimes the wasps and bees in the eaves of the barn would return to their hives at twilight and how the barn hummed with the vibration of their settling. He was not a poet. He told the story simply and yet she longed to hear the fragrant wood humming.

On the night of the blue trout he had touched her shoulder, only that, and showed her the high window at the end of the apple barn, a small square near the peak of the third story where by happenchance the moon had framed itself in the opening.

"Once I saw a crescent moon hold Venus in her arms," he said.

She was surprised at what she would have done in the darkness and perfume of the apple barn on the night of the blue trout. Despite the warmth she felt within, she bid him thanks and left, shivering in the summer night and the setting moon.

Now they came back intently, at her bidding. She was dressed in yellow cotton with a white half-slip under. She wore the same brown sandals. She asked him to tell about the bees again.

"I'm not really much of a storyteller," he said, surprisingly embarrassed. "I'd be afraid to spoil it in the retelling."

"Is this what you want?" he asked. She had touched him. He touched her, gently on the cheek.

"I don't know," she said, "I seem to. I came to you."

He made a nest and they held each other. Not the foul nest of the heron but a nest of blankets topped with an old quilt , all of them dragged out from the little office at the end of the apple barn together with a bottle of white wine which smelled faintly of apples once it was uncorked.

"You keep bedding here," she said simply.

"Now and again someone sleeps here," he said. "Not always what you think."

She begged him for the bees.

"There's a low sound everywhere like there is sometimes if you put your ear to a tree in the middle of a woods somewhere."

Did he do this? Yes.

After making love in the apple warehouse on the night of the blue heron, she told him their embraces were an anthology. "The word actually means a garland of flowers," she said.

"Does it?" he said. She wasn't certain whether he was being ironic.

It was a sweet time. The strangest thing was the way his ass felt, narrow as flint but with the roundedness of the exposed wood of a curved tree limb where the bark has worn away. Noah's rump was a firm round muscle, power and substance and soft solidity.

And in the midst of it all she was aware of the old woman, not there with them of course, but close, in the house, like the fragrance of apples, the buzzing wood, the distant moon. A woman who had raised daughters, how sad it was, she in the house and her son out back riding the girl. How sad it was that life could come to this. Soon she too would fall and dry, the little leather purses of dried apples, the thin white bones within thin white arms. All women would fall and dry, all women did and it was exceedingly sad, even then.

She wouldn't let Paul kiss her when she left the barn, not out of any particular sense of shame but circumspection. She promised to see him again.

Back home, but not home, at the Italian language institute, she missed Noah terribly. Really. Deeply. Certainly. Him.

Certo. Sempre.

CHAPTER FOUR

Fond of the Light

As soon as the power was back on, Antoinette insisted on making him dinner. "I won't hear of you eating alone on a night when your wife is gone and your son has set off," she said. "There's a chicken in the freezer and I can roast it."

She had proceeded to tear the frozen chicken free from its plastic wrapping and then picked free the little bits of paper diaper where they adhered between the chicken and the chicken-colored styrofoam tray. Meanwhile she lit the oven and cranked it up to five hundred and fifty degrees while she covered her hands in olive oil and massaged the frozen chicken. What looked like a splayed and butterflied chicken turned out under her hands to be a mass of frozen chicken parts adhered into a flattened, cubist bird. This mass of bird she salted and peppered mightily and then threw a few sprigs of fresh rosemary on top of it and put the whole sprawl on a baking tray.

"Later we'll bathe the poor thing in lemon juice," she said, "to cool it down from the initial searing while the oven cools for the real roasting. An hour or so more and we'll have our roast. We can pass the time with gin and tonic."

Every division is a space for something, Noah thought.

"I admire your wife's poetry," she said out of nowhere, "I probably shouldn't tell you this but that's half of why I chose you to do my trust."

"And the other half?" he asked.

"You remind me of someone," she said, not without mischief.

She asked him to set up a folding table in the swimming pool. He asked her again to be certain. "Yes," she laughed. "The old pool. You'll think I'm dafter than you already do, I know, but I'm fond of the light and the feel there."

He had not expected her to seem in any way sexual and yet she was in a way that almost made him uncomfortable. She wore a summer shift of Shaker cotton bought a half century before from a Shaker woman she used to visit. It was the milky blue color of certain skies.

She had used that phrase, "a half century ago," not exactly in the way someone would say yesterday, not so unaware and yet not uncomfortable with that base of numeration. She spoke century in a world of yesterday just as some spoke decimal in a world of binary.

"I'm one short of everything, as the old Irishman said of his two-legged milking stool."

There was something bawdy there because she reddened and laughed although Noah didn't quite understand the joke.

"I was born short," she said, still laughing. "Nineteen and ten put me one short of ten when we came here, one short of nineteen and twenty. I'm five feet five or was before my back bent, one short of another half. I'll be ninety in ninety-nine, a year short of the millennium."

"That can't be right," Noah blurted. "If you were nine in nineteen that would make you ninety in two thousand."

"Men are hopeless with numbers," she said, patting his cheek familiarly and beginning to whistle.

She was starting to like having him there he thought, her hand against his cheek had been soft as powder and oddly sensual.

The song she whistled was called the Derry air.

"Do you know it?" she asked. "It's an old joke. Do you know the Derry air? Do you get it?"

He got it. Derriere.

The question of the light had been more complicated than he had thought it would be at first. It wasn't the fuses circuit breakers really he had been surprised to see, someone had kept up with the infrastructure, new copper risers also in the basement.

He was about to call Niagara Mohawk to check the service when Mrs. Ryan, Antoinette she had insisted by then, suggested he take a run down to the screen house to see if there was light there.

"Normally I'd have gone there by now," she said. "To paint and take in the light and air. But I woke feeling damp and arthritic, too achy really to walk down there until my pills kick in."

She laughed.

"Kick in or kick start me, who can say?"

"Not me," he said and she had liked that.

There was power to the screen house he found out as soon as he reached it and tested the porch lights. On his way back to the main house he circled round and looked for where the service dropped. There was an exterior main there, normally padlocked, the lock left open long ago enough that lock and hasp were both thoroughly rusted. The main had been pulled by someone, something, a small tuft of coarse hair snagged on the sharp edge.

"What is it?" she asked.

"Deer, I think," he said.

"Isn't that extraordinary?" she said. "Some sort of sign."

"Sign?"

"That you should be here," she said.

"Dear," she said. "Deer, dear," laughing to see him so flustered.

He felt his feelings hurt. Apparently showed it.

"I'm really sorry," she said. "You think I'm quite mad, don't you? You have what? three or four dealings with someone you are setting up an ordinary trust for and then she's there on your telephone machine, lost and ancient. Poor dear…"

"Aren't you worried being here alone?" he asked.

She really inhabited no more than a hut in the village of the great house: kitchen and parlor and above the kitchen a back bedroom once maid's quarters, with a Spartan bed and a single watercolor of iris, her own work, in a twig frame.

"I haven't needed more bed than that in ten years," she said a little naughtily.

Ninety minus ten was eighty minus one was.

"You are moving your lips," she said.

"What's that?"

"Counting I suspect."

"I'm sorry," he said.

"Don't be. Men always are. Oops—" she said, it was unexpectedly charming, anachronistic, to hear her oops. "Oops, I shouldn't have said that. Shouldn't have said any of it."

Now they were sitting in candlelight within the roofless walls of the mossy enclosure of the old swimming pool, having descended there via a sloping set of four wide concrete stairs at the shallow end and proceeded in an almost courtly procession to the deeper end where earlier at her bidding he had set up the folding card table and covered it with linen and silver and hand-painted china for their picnic, putting new candles in the drain inlets which served, more than once before, as candle sconces.

Once they were seated it almost made sense to be there. It was less a bunker than a sunken patio, a valley in which the slant light of dusk already no longer reached and yet still arched over them like a lavender and salmon awning.

"I love the way the candle light plays along these walls and how the concrete amplifies the birdsong," she said.

"I'm happy to be here," he said.

"Are you really?" she asked, "are you really?"

Much later in the afternoon he remembered that he had wanted to remember more about the French woman.

The third time, the worst meeting, was easiest to remember.

He had wanted to see her alone and in sunlight for no real reason except to see her so. It was a plan no hardly a plan, an impulse, an impulse he formed sometime late in the second long meeting the three of them had under the pine trees.

It was nearly dawn, they had talked all night, about this and that, buoyed by the pure fact of the second meeting and the ability to summon some resumption. It was flirtier and funny and even a little wild. She was their angel, their earth mother before they knew that word. They had talked of dreams and stars and ancient wars and he could see the glimmer no the smudge, the brightening smudge of dawn behind them.

Pete went off to piss behind the trees. They each had pissed there, even her, from time to time that night. She'd brought red wine in a string bag and water in a green Girl Scout's canteen slung around her neck like a purse. It was clear that she was hoping they were there again, clear she was planning to talk. The first time when she excused herself to slip away he saw her duck behind the tree and squat, lifting her skirts, before, embarrassed, he looked away. It wasn't that unusual, they traveled in a fairly enlightened crowd, girls from the Seminary who slipped out of clothes and into bathing suits under long bath towels, girls who would on a lark jump out of a car and squat in the shelter of a car door to drain off beer.

Even so this was different and he and Pete kept silent while she was away from them, as if afraid to say something that would seem disrespectful. As a result they heard the rustle of water, like mice scurrying, in the grass.

Then when Pete was away behind the trees Noah asked her to meet him sometime in daylight.

"Aren't you worried what your friend will think?"

"We're not your boyfriends," he said sharply.

"Aren't you?" she asked and playfully touched his cheek. Her touch scalded and she saw him recoil from it.

"I'm sorry," she said. "*Désolée…*"

He felt terribly exposed and shamed.

"You Americans, you are so tender," she said, "I forget. I've been through war, I'm hard as rusk."

She touched his cheek again and she somehow managed to make her hand like ice against the burning.

"You see that bookstore over there?" she pointed through the trees and across Main Street, "I will meet you there tomorrow afternoon at three sharp. I'll bring you violets."

"Violets?" Pete said, stepping back, "or violins?"

"I'll bring *you* violins, cher Pierre," she said, and touched his cheek as well, watching Noah's eyes all the time.

"I lived in Spain," Antoinette was saying. "For fifteen years I lived in Spain. La Costa del Sol, do you know where that is? Costa is both coast and cost in Spanish, a very economical language, wouldn't you say? The cost of light was high on La Costa del Sol believe me…"

The chicken was delicious, improbably impossibly moist after almost two hours on low heat following the first half hour's spattering, smoking, crackling time in the hottest oven. For the last hour or more she had introduced parsnips to the oven and the smallest potatoes, both now dipped into a shared bowl of melted butter set between them. Salad would follow, greens from a small garden outside the door of her kitchen hut.

Noah had not been there long before he realized he knew relatively nothing about her despite the fact that he thought he knew the most intimate details of her means and her holdings, her charitable and philanthropic interests, her family or lack thereof.

"If you don't mind my asking," he asked, "I wonder why you called me. Isn't there anyone else?"

"When you live to be ninety even the caretaker retires," she said. "To Florida no less," she laughed then looked him in the eye. "Sometimes living on is a bother."

"We continue or cease," he said wisely.

"It's a good man who can quote his wife's poetry," she said.

It was an embarrassment, he had forgotten that Cathleen used it in a poem. Forgotten in fact whether the first time she said it to him was before or after she had written the poem.

"This is delicious," he said.

"Bistro food," she said. "A painter's meal. Or did you mean this conversation?"

In the candlelight and after wine the splotches of her puppet cheeks were softer above her smile, delicate and ancient as the poster for a music hall chanteuse.

The French woman in daylight on the other hand was rawer. Too beautiful to see directly, almost hideous outside the darkness. He had waited an hour for her to show up, half an hour early and the thirty minutes she was late.

"In Paree I am early," she said, really saying the name like that. Gay Paree. "*Une demi heure est a l'heure,*" she said.

He knew what it meant, he wasn't a fool.

She handed him a small clay pot with violets.

"We are not in Paree, are we?" he said stupidly, not knowing what to do with the pot, already feeling that the whole idea was a blunder.

"*Non, cherie,*" she said, maddeningly insisting on more French than she ever used with them in darkness.

He was afraid she would touch his cheek again.

Instead she looked around him at the books.

"You have an interest in mechanical engineering?" she laughed.

He hadn't known where to wait for her, moving from the drama shelves (his favorites then) to poetry to art to the textbook shelves nearest the door when it became later and later.

"Do you want to go somewhere?" she asked.

He hadn't thought of this, had no idea beyond seeing her, and that idea now seemed a tired memory of a sleepless night.

"We could go up to the columns, I suppose," he said.

"It would spoil that, wouldn't it?" she asked.

He was glad she said that.

"What did you imagine?" she asked gently enough that it should not have hurt him so.

"I didn't, damn it," he snapped, mad that she had been so late and more so that he did not know. "I imagined nothing. I don't know why I asked."

"Just to see if you could moved me?" she asked, getting the verb wrong. She pointed to the books just beyond his shoulder where he faced her, "Mechanical engineering? A body in motion, a body in rest?"

He ran away then. It was stupid, he was still a teenager, still so full of anger, some of which had never seemed to leave him. It seemed an appropriate gesture in the face of her words, a body in motion. It was the only gesture, he knew now, that he could have made in the face of her beauty. He ran across Main Street and the huge sloping lawn of the university, running toward the columns and the pines, and then stopped short, hurling the clay pot of violets like a grenade, tumbling in the sunlight.

He mourned her like a dead creature, yet some strand of life kept her alive in his memory just as the French priest Cathleen had told him about had said.

಼ಲ ಼ಲ

Antoinette Mulvey sailed away with her brother in the company of an aunt, sailing to the new world and away from death.

"We were technically orphans," she said, "Mum and dad dead
of influenza in the great epidemic of 1918. Even so there were
relations enough beyond my dear aunt if we had wanted to stay
in Ireland. It was just that so much was lost we couldn't see to
stay, you know. It was like the famine all over again for us, seventy years after, the second diaspora."

The light was fading quickly now and her melodious voice
echoed in the odd concrete cave where they had eaten. She was
telling her story.

She told him as much: "I'm going to tell you my story now
and be done with it. Not just done with it for you but done
with it all together, if you understand me. There's less and less
audience left to tell it to and more and more left to tell…"

Cathleen would have found just the right thing to say to comfort her, Noah knew, but he couldn't think of anything.

"Now now…" he said and the noise of it seemed a comfort,
to him at least if not to her.

"I spent fifteen years on the Costa del Sol and took my last
lover when I was seventy-nine years old and then came back here
because I knew I would never have my health quite the same
again, so I'm pretty certain I know the end of things," she said.

Noah sat and listened to her without making any noise.

"It's strange to think now but another few years and my
brother and I might never have come to America at all, what
with the peace in twenty-two and the way they clamped down
on immigration not long after. Surely we never would have come

as two orphans with a bag of money and a dead auntie slid down beneath the sea behind us. It wouldn't have been possible, I suppose. I'm still not sure how my brother talked us into the care of old Crotty and down to Pennsylvania, god bless him."

They weren't exactly traveling steerage, despite being orphans, though they weren't dining with the captain either. Their aunt had means of her own, she'd sons who were policemen in New York and she had been saving the money they sent back to her and which she carried in a satchel. Then a third of the way across the Atlantic she died of pleurisy.

"Whatever happened to pleurisy, do you suppose?" Antoinette asked. "I suppose it's all gotten folded into pneumonia and more scientific sounding diseases. There was always something woefully comforting about the name of pleurisy. It's a word that sounds like crying."

To Noah every word sounded like crying then.

"Should we take these things in?" he asked softly.

"I suppose," she said, pulling the large basket from the corner and beginning to stuff it with the china and the leftovers, "but you'll have to promise you'll come down to the screen house with me to hear the end of the story."

She looked at him, not sadly but directly.

"You're the only audience left," she said.

Noah knew that magic gathered sometimes like how balls of quicksilver would find each other and consolidate if you shook them on a tray. Cathleen had come into his life like this at a time when it could have been anything it was so scattered, so silver, like the stars of an expanding universe.

He had begun on the wrong foot, so to speak, when they first met, somehow absurdly talking to her about British shoes and how good they were. He was very proud of his suits and shoes in those days. How could she ever have tolerated him? A prig is defined as a junior partner.

And she was an angel in saffron and he talked her into leaving the party at the cottage and then watched as she slipped the beach dress up and off over her head for that moment turning the crowded beach silent and empty and then she let him take her hand over the stones near the shore.

After their swim they went back up to the cottage and baked bread together and fell in love in the sultry afternoon. It was a lark and had struck everyone as mad. He remembered her hands patting the elastic loaves, remembered her breasts and thighs in the black bathing suit under the saffron beach dress, remembered as if it were yesterday.

As if it were a mere half century.

They believed in angels long before angels became a commodity. On the trip to Spoleto which was and was not their honeymoon there was man in Florence who asked if they were lost and they said they were looking for the Ufizi and he led them to a small church off a square where there was no one else and the gray marble floors danced with light from the windows and Christ ascended into the light and gold and glory in some magnificent Donatello painting, neither the church nor the painting mentioned in their guidebooks, and the man gone when they turned to thank him. Later in Spoleto they saw a play in which everyone was nude and gleaming with olive oil and that same night they too laved themselves and gleamed like serpents.

He knew love, he knew angels and serpents and how the stars consolidate into a single light, yet the conjunction of Antoinette Ryan and his memories of the French woman blindsided him.

"They say angels come to you when the universe finds you wanting," Cathleen had said that day in Florence.

Noah wanted so much now. A future for their son and a sense of what they would become with him gone away, for starters.

Antoinette was his angel for this day. After she showed him all the rooms of the first floor of the house with their furniture and lamps shrouded like ghosts, she was quite weary, so much so he suggested that they stay in the kitchen instead of walking down to the screen house as she wanted.

"You promised," she said.

"I promised to hear your story."

"My story depends on the screen house. It's really where I live here in this season. It's where my memories live."

It took them a long while to walk down from the house. At first Noah considered offering to carry her on his back like Saint Christopher. But she knew her way here in every way, knew the path like deer do (they saw four of them midway down to the lake and the screen house after he had showed her the deer fur earlier Antoinette told him that during the rut she sometimes heard them brush against the house in the night like wind). She knew her body in both its frailties and its strengths.

"I walk like a goat," she said, and laughed. "An old goat you could say. It's bones that do you in at my age. One day I'll stumble and my hip will shatter and they'll find my broken bones years later strewn along this path and shining like chalk."

"I have no sense of what someone ninety years old can do."

"How naughty of you," Antoinette laughed. "Seriously though, it's all tribal after all. In Ireland our people were sheep herders and the old women would go out onto the hillsides well into their nineties, pulling lambs from their mothers lest they be stillborn, their arms sunk into the bloody wombs and their heads raised up against the rain storms. You live into your old age the way you were planted. Our stock was gnarled but strong. I'll die of my own doing."

"You mean…?"

She looked up at him mischievously, she was holding his arm now down the steeper part of the path, tiny as a jewel she was.

I mean what I mean," she said. "I'm not talking about hemlock or the gun and I couldn't imagine sitting with my head in the oven like that poor girl the poet. I mean we all die of our own death. At first we let it happen to us and then we cling to it like a long-awaited lover."

How could she know this, Noah wondered.

"Take my poor Aunt Eveline," she said. "Surely you were struck by the fact that at least this one Irish woman from such a sheep-herding line, not to mention my own poor mother, fell before her time. The truth is, I feel sure now, my aunt couldn't bear to leave her country and couldn't not go to her children, her flat-footed boyos. It's what the anthropologist called the double-bind. We die of it, all of us, bound up in life and leaving it alike."

"Did you want to have children?" Noah asked.

He felt her lapse a second at his elbow, like a sack of flour slips a moment in your grasp and then you hold it up again.

"I wanted everything once," she said.

"I'm sorry," he said but she waved him off.

"We had one before Ryan died and it was born dead, white as marble and soft as the moon, with a head of black hair you would never believe. I couldn't have one after then."

He squeezed her arm, it seemed the right thing to do.

"And your son?" she asked.

"His hair is blond," Noah said, then realized that wasn't quite appropriate. "He's like an angel, I mean. We're going to miss him."

He was surprised to feel his voice hitch, almost in tears. Antoinette for her part squeezed his arm in return.

They were nearing the lake and the screen house now and the darkness was settling like a scrim of gray and a loon was calling somewhere.

"My brother, god bless him, was blond as a Rory," she said.

Noah had to ask her the word, he thought she said roaring.

"God knows where that's from," she said. "I've heard the saying as long as I remember. Who knows but there might have been some traveling Scotsman once who crowned certain children of the village with his pale mark, don't you know."

She looked up at him as if testing, mischievous again.

"It was sometimes more than sheep in labor brought the women out into the hills then," she said.

"Still is," he said without thinking, then wondered, for the first time in some time, whether Cathleen had ever had an affair.

"My brother had the Scot in him as far as business goes," Antoinette said. "When my auntie was dying we found a priest somewhere all those days on the boat, and even the days before it, are a smear of memory to me now; they've always been really, I was only nine years you have to remember and I swear the priest had hardly finished anointing her when the brother returns with old Crotty in hand and announces that he's agreed to sponsor us. I suspect it took a little bit of the stuffing from auntie's satchel to convince Crotty to do his good works, but not much that's for sure. My brother had enough left to build an empire. You're walking in it now, Mr. Williams, you are walking in it now, god love him…"

Noah was trying to think of Cathleen in someone else's arms but the thought didn't make sense and his heart ached and they were blessedly at the screen house. Even so he could imagine her white flanks and her white arms and someone's dark hand moving over the white curves of her back and shoulders.

"What is your name again?" Pete had asked the French woman when she came upon them the second time and she said Claire de Lune.

"What's yours?" she asked laughing, settling her things on the same column where she had sat the last time.

"Buggs Bunny," Pete said.

"I said Claire de Lune not Loony Tunes," the French women retorted. "Anyway you are a camel *pas du lapin*, what with your camel color hair and your big shoulder…"

She pronounced it *couleur* and said only one shoulder like the French Canadians did. He brought these memories up through the years the way someone dives for smooth colored stones. What she said would have stuck with him anyway maybe but it was so remarkable in so many ways to have her back again when they almost thought they imagined her the first time, to have such a woman tease with you, right from the start let alone at all on the second meeting, that he sealed it in his memory.

"What's Noah then?" Pete asked.

The French woman regarded him. She had lifted herself up onto the sawn column, swinging her rear end up and back between two arms like a trapeze artist, and now she looked at Noah and fumbled with the bottle of wine she had brought.

"Such sad eyes," she said. "Those dark, sad eyes and that broad brow can only be what do you call it, *l'âne?*"

She looked to Pete for the French, he didn't know the word.

"Donkey," Noah said. "Thanks very much."

He guffawed, the French woman was a nut. She had chased down two boys she met once and brought along a picnic and a canteen. Screw her, she could take off and they'd be just fine.

"You are hurt," she said, "but this means something different to you than it does to me. I call you the donkey named Patience, it is a good name, a good being, strong and wise..."

It wasn't the first time he had been so baptized, he wore strength like a burden for almost as long as he could remember. For almost that long he longed to be sometimes at least numbered among the weak, someone who could depend on others, find his solace in others' dark eyes and others' patience. It wasn't what he was given to. He was a donkey named Patience.

Antoinette was napping in the rocking chair. Hers was a screen house with more emphasis on house than screen, a square Adirondack style cottage with a high sloping roof, the house two thirds of the square and the screened verandah the other, or perhaps a little more considering that it wrapped around two sides of the house, lake side and low meadow. He went back out onto the porch when he saw her sleeping.

"Don't you dare leave me without my story," she said, opening one eye.

"I'll watch the lake for a while," he whispered.

She closed her eye but spoke again softly.

"There will be Perseids tonight," she said. "Sometimes you can see the reflections of them etched upon the water."

"Rest," he said, and she did.

Already there were stars floating on the water and dark creatures, bats most likely, swooping low. A fish splashed and the ripple rose up like an embossment. Noah believed he spied an occasional lightning bug along the shore grass though he was certain they must be out of season. He was certain the Perseids were also. He remembered helping Liam gather lightning bugs much earlier in long-ago summers, slipping the bugs into a mayonnaise jar whose lid Noah had perforated with a screwdriver, watching the slowing glow of them as they slipped down into the choke of grass which Liam, like all children, insisted on putting in the jar with them, despite the fact that there was no evidence that lightning bugs prospered with it or even depended upon it.

In the dark of the porch he saw the light upon the water through watery eyes. It would be crazy to cry, really, they had not lost him but rather brought him to the point they imagined for him from when he was first with them, an infant with hinged and springing legs like a cricket when you stood him in your lap. We knew then he would one day walk away, Noah thought, recalling Liam's shy wave when he and Cathleen left to drive away downstate.

Now she was coming back without him, coming back without quite coming back.

"Mr. Williams?" Antoinette called from the inner room, "will you have tea?"

Sometime in her long life she had learned the secret of silent movement, moving to and from rooms, in and out of sleep, like a leaf on the wind. Perhaps she had merely shrunk away into lightness, he thought, sloughing off every heavy thing.

Though not the heaviness of memory, he knew.

They resumed her story inside sitting at the hand-hewn table. The big room, as she called it, was furnished with a quartet of rocking chairs and a long bent-twig camelback sofa with a Hudson Bay blanket folded over it like a red and yellow flag. Opposite the sofa was a fireplace hearth high enough for a stooped man to walk into and wide enough to fit a small car through. There was a tea kettle hanging from a hook which swung over the fire which she slipped off the hook and placed on a single burner electric hot plate at the end of the table. They sat for a while listening to the water rattle in the pot on the hot plate. Before long it began to sigh and Antoinette went to a cupboard and retrieved a china teapot. Leaning against the hearth was a basket for making popcorn like the one he and Cathleen had for their fireplace.

"I could roast an ox here if I had an ox," Antoinette said.

"You should have a phone," he said.

"Do you need to make another call?" she asked, an edge of concern in her voice.

"I mean in case of emergency," he said.

"Yes counselor," she parried and poured the now whistling water into a teapot which had the strangest scene painted on it, a girl in a field of flowers and fire.

"My teapot's caught your eye, I see," she said. "It's something of a visual prank, my work I'm afraid, a little acerbic jest from long ago days. That's Persephone in hell, it seemed the right subject for a domestic object."

Something else caught his eye. Across the room on the wall opposite the lakeside there was a small oil painting in blues and the faintest yellow green, a landscape like a faded lapis lazuli. Though of land, it spoke of water and seemed exactly right there, so extraordinary that the whole room seemed to float toward it.

He walked over to view it more closely. Fields and narrow trees, yellow light like a straightedge, a curved path below a rising mound which subtly rhymed with its contours.

"That makes the trip up and down the hill with me each season," she said. "It summers here, in winter it takes the place of the iris in my bedroom. You like it?"

At first he thought she meant a trip up and down the mound in the painting.

"I love it," he said. "Yours?"

She had moved silently to him again, stood by his shoulder and looked at the painting with him.

"In what sense?" she asked.

It was a curious question and the way she asked it he knew instantly she meant something else by it.

"If you mean in the sense that's it's mine because I painted it, I'm flattered."

"Yes," he said.

"But if you mean is it mine in the sense of possession, yes I own it, though in the first sense and all other senses including that last it's Cezanne's."

"Jesus," he said.

"Yes," she said, "sometimes he seems to be that to me."

It was a small joke and she smiled.

Noah turned to her.

"Of course you know—"

"It's worth as much as all the rest of my estate combined…?" she finished his sentence.

"Yes," he said again.

"In that sense it's worthless to me," she said. "Worthless or priceless, it's all the same. Do you want it? I'll give it to you."

"Of course I would want it, anyone would," he said, a little snappish now. Despite the pleasant time they had managed to have thus far, it wasn't really established that she still wasn't a little addled.

"That's not the point," he said.

"Oh but it is," she said. "That's what makes an art object. I could give it to you or to a mechanic in town. Or I could just as well walk down to the dock one night and skim it out across the water and give it to eternity. Some things can't be accounted for in your trusts, Mr. Williams. Let's have our tea, why don't we."

She gestured toward the table.

"Why don't you sit where you can see the painting."

She poured the tea from the Persephone pot and faint steeped flowers slid into the cup, blue flowers and softly faded hay colored ones, a floral tea.

"Now you'll want to know the story backwards and so I'll tell you about the Cezanne first because it's as easy an entry into where the money came from and my darling Scotch brother Rory Mulvey as any other…"

She had come awake with the catnap and the tea and her white skin glowed like a cameo above the Shaker shift and the white Irish wool shawl she had pulled around her to walk to the screen house.

"There's not a lot to it, really," she said. "We knew what it was, we knew pretty well better than many others around us what Cezanne was. By 1933 when the rest of the world was deep in the great depression, my brother Brian that was Rory's real name, you know was wealthy and getting wealthier. What he owned was real, he always said, he had real estate and others lost their shirts on dreams. Meanwhile people always liked a roof over their heads, even in the midst of the depression—especially then and a hotel man never suffered if he didn't owe anyone money."

"Did he go into the hotel business as soon as you landed?" Noah asked.

She sipped her tea and smiled, drawing the tea up in a slurping breath like the Chinese did, cooling it with her breath.

"In a sense, yes," she said. "He was a bootblack at Crotty's hotel in Scranton, Pennsylvania and I was a housemaid."

"But the satchel of money?" he asked.

"Mr. Williams," she said. "You go at stories as if they were a lawsuit. All you lawyers wish to be writers but you wish the world were simpler than it is."

"Noah," he said, feeling slightly chastised.

"Dear Noah," she said, sounding exactly like Cathleen, "I truly don't mean to talk harshly after you have been so very kind—"

She stopped as if she had just thought of something.

"You are aptly named, aren't you Noah? It seems clear that you are something of a world saver, fussing the world aboard your ark, every creature by twos, all your wonderful caring swamped by your arithmetic."

She looked directly at him.

"Who will save you, Noah, while you're busy saving everyone else?"

Cathleen, he wanted to say, Cathleen, but he could not find his voice.

The French woman had three children of her own, one of them dead. What was a story if it wasn't that? It was all the same, wasn't it? There were greater and lesser details, great lawns and lower lawns, main houses and screen houses, hills that rhymed with curves, masterpieces sunk like shining stones at the bottom of dark ponds, their gilt frames like upturned eyes through which sailed the reflections of comets overhead.

He had told Cathleen about the Frenchwoman, but it was long ago and long before either Cathleen or the Frenchwoman had become whom they had become. Indeed, he didn't know until today. Still, it was surprising how little he had told her.

It was the kind of story she should know, the kind of story he would want her to know. He told her everything. Which is what he would have told someone who came to know him well enough to know about his wife, someone at the gym for instance or over martinis. I tell her everything. We tell each other everything.

It was impossible of course. Barely possible to tell the smallest thing before a story seemed to melt away. You would begin certain there was so much to say and then, not halfway in, find yourself already there, suddenly at the place that you were so certain when you started would take so much time and require such complex paths to reach. Even if you did manage to move along through the paths you first imagined, when you did finally get there the person you were telling it to would think you were somewhere else.

Life, he knew—oh he knew this much at least from a life with Cathleen—was trying nonetheless. Trying to reach a place in common, trying to find words to fit a space.

She was right, Antoinette was, despite its reputation for needless complexity law made the world briefly simpler than it was. The Cezanne was no different, light distilled into lime and citron, a muscled hump of soft green. Sex likewise.

Still we know nothing of each other finally, he thought. If you asked her about the French woman, with some prompting—remember the story Noah told you about when he was a teen, just before he went away to college? Cathleen would recall it as a midsummer story of adolescent infatuation and a young man's introduction to loss. The name of the story was the commonplace of certain domestic tragedies. Babies are born and die, children live or fail, ring around the rosy, we all fall down.

All through law school Noah had loved another woman and still sent her Christmas cards every year in San Francisco thanks to Cathleen's list which remembered it for him. There were photos of her on the alcove wall of their bedroom. She had a name but ever since Liam had asked who it was some years ago there wasn't any reason to utter it except for the Christmas card list or an occasional mention of her in the law school alumni quarterly. She, too, had daughters and once in a sort of foolish reckoning he had tried to count up for himself how many times they might have made love.

Figure three times a week on average even for a young man, accounting for weeks away and weeks on end spent largely distracted or weary or in the library. Times fifty two was (why was this so hard to do?) one fifty six, times three was four hundred and fifty-something.

With Cathleen it would be close to three thousand.

Yet he knew nothing for certain of either of them. They say you cannot remember sensations, no memory of pain but the occasion of pain, the same seemingly true of pleasure. It meant nothing. He did not surmise from this that the flesh told us nothing, but rather that what we know of the flesh is no different than what we know otherwise.

We marry each other's secrets as well as our knowledges, Noah thought. If the truth be told, what he and Cathleen knew of each other was surely less than what they did not know even though he knew they knew more of each other than almost anyone.

They told each other everything.

"Are you an actress?" Noah had asked the French woman sometime in that second meeting.

"*Peut-être*, like any woman, *quelquefois*."

Perhaps. Sometimes. She tested his patience ever since he surprised her knowing the word for donkey.

"Do I look like an actress?" she teased him, her voice a little sultry on a sultry night.

"You look like a circus performer," he said, "a trapeze artist."

"Whoa!" Pete laughed. "Got you!"

"All done up in sequins and spinning," she said softly. "I told you, I'm Claire de Lune."

"What do you want here?" Noah asked her. "Why chase after us?"

She was always hurting him, he realized now, decades too belatedly. In those days he was ripe with obscure hurts and just about anyone could pluck them from him. Liam was the same way sometimes, although decades later and with Cathleen as his mother not as blind to his own hurts as Noah had been.

"You mean like butterflies?" the French woman asked and sighed. "I miss my children," she said, the response an obscure hurt to him.

For some people, mostly men he acknowledged, hurts pushed out like a bunch of grapes and you couldn't handle them without bruising.

"So we are children to you?" he confronted her.

"Don't be absurd," she said, bruising him still more.

"My daughter is *cinq ans*, my poor moth of a son only two and his mother gone away over the seas."

"What makes your son poor?" he persisted.

You could see it coming, anyone could. Pete did.

"Come on," he said. "Lay off the twenty questions, okay?"

Pete was a camel, six feet six inches tall, his shoulders a four foot beam as he walked among the columns in a figure eight, yellow hair gleaming on his dromedary head.

They had become a circus for an instant. Noah the ring master with his black britches and whistle, the French woman on the high wire in a sequined leotard.

She descended.

"I lost a son, my baby, two years ago and the same year my youngest son was born. That makes him and all of us poor, my friend. Now he and his sister are with their grandmother while I am here and their father is god knows where. Do you want to know more?"

"No," he whispered. Pete stopped the circle eight and watched them. The circus ended.

"Even so I will tell you more," she said. "First of all because you are still a boy—forgive me if that hurts you—as much as you are a man, I will tell you more so that you do not think life and death are so simple. Then because you are an American, because you both are, forgive you—" she laughed nervously, "I will tell you more so that you do not think all life everywhere is without history."

She began to weave through the columns, slowly, consciously, making the same spiral that Pete had made but turning the circle eight into a labyrinth as she talked.

"My mother was a midwife so I've seen life and death. My husband was away at war when our first son died. My mother lost her house in the same war. The year our baby died my brother was condemned to death for supporting independence in our home country. The year my second son turned one years old independence came and yet the same brother and my mother were arrested and, although she stayed while he fled home when I managed to have them freed, she was eventually expelled by her own government, and became what you call in America, a woman without a country. Her only country the body of woman. She lives near me."

She was still weaving spirals. The history was a spiral. It made no sense. It made complete sense.

"What happened to your brother?" Pete asked her. He had

begun to make the circle eights again, following after her.

She laughed delightedly.

"He lives happily ever after," she said. "He is a baby's doctor, his mother's son, how do you say a *pédiatre?*"

He had told this part of the story of the French woman to Cathleen once one night in the early months when she was pregnant with Liam. She was worried that he would die on them, die in the womb, because for the whole of the day before she could not feel him moving.

In the story he told Cathleen there were no spirals and no circus and in its telling it became as much a story of Pete Ehmer's death and the end of childhood as it was a story of magic and summer and the Frenchwoman.

"This all sounds vaguely familiar to me," Cathleen had said. "As if you told it to me once before."

She had snuggled against him and thanked him for calming her, a curious thing really given how much death there was in what he had said. She was still worried, he knew, he could hear it in her breathing. He counted her breaths and the intervals between them, as worried as she was about their baby though he dare not tell her that, waiting with her until her breathing slowly slowed into sleep. And when the interval between the breaths matched their duration he matched the rhythm of his own breaths to hers, following her as he fell.

She woke him in the darkness a few hours afterwards to whisper that she had just felt the baby move Liam or Leila, the names they had for them. It was the middle of the night and these were the days before knowing the sex of babies, the days before Cathleen came to know in a way she could not explain to

Noah that the child within her, Liam, was a boy and they bade his imaginary other, the child named Leila, a silent farewell, a child without a story, a daughter as lost as any.

CHAPTER FIVE

Storm

H e was back in the front seat next to her again. In the late morning light the procession from echo to butter to storm lay in memory like an only partially retrieved dream. From memory likewise she knew the light on the fair hairs along the curve of the earlobe, and the touch of the soft, slim fingers of the man next to her, whom she would see never again and who by way of farewell showed her the mountain, its names, and phases.

Storm was the mountain's last name, as any mountain's she supposed.

Twenty years had passed yet sometimes in this journey she thought she might see him on the road in the traffic coming toward them.

It became clear to her that, even before their brief clash and his retreat to the back seat, Liam was in a desperate funk. He was impatient and prickly from sometime after lunch and it built on the way over the mountain. Their contretemps about the meaning of his childhood stories and the reveries which followed for her were only a continuance.

She didn't like the mountain's other shoulder, the thunder, though it was no less beautiful. Southward it slipped into the

West Point reservation and the road was bordered with great oaks from time to time. It was as if something was over. A pickup truck with an NRA sticker on the rear windshield and assorted patriotic bumper stickers punctuated this emotion. The boy at the wheel was a rabbity thin head-banger with frail yellow hair down the middle of his shoulders, in some way the antithesis of Liam, in another linked by a headstrong attempt to mask fears and vulnerability in a grim and endlessly touching silence.

All of us sitting above the roadside in invisible metal cages, conveyed by magnetism or upon the cushion of air of a hovercraft, legs stretched before us, vulnerable as nested birds.

She tried the idea out on him. It was a sacrificial gesture. He could teethe away his fear and anger on the soft leather of her foolishness. It worked.

"What in the world are you talking about!" he exploded, yet laughing despite himself. "Magnets or hovercraft! God, you are so strange sometimes…"

"It's as likely an explanation as tires carrying us," she said, smiling back. "What proof do you have of that? Strip all the steel away and there we all are, sitting in the air."

It was an old game, a mother's tease, a bedtime story.

"You can see the other cars," he said. "There's the proof."

"Wheels go backwards in some movies," she said.

"Oh my god, you've lost your mind," he said. "The road's made you whacko!"

"It's like Shakespeare said about lovemaking," she said, treading truly whacko ground now. "Strip it all away—the tires, the magnets, and the cushion of air—and everyone is just wrestling."

He suddenly said something surprising.

"It's not just men, you know, who look foolish, it's girls too."

Teasing, Liam spoke with a curious vehemence, as if she threatened something in what she had said, and she supposed she did, thus explaining the other curiosity of his retort, the unbalanced parallelism of his complaint: in which he said not men and women, but men and girls.

Was this what was on his mind?

"Of course it's not just men," she said. "Did I say that? I didn't mean to say that. I wouldn't say that. I didn't say that," she said laughing. "It's all the same for boys and women and women and women and women and girls and boys and men and men. We're all polywogs in sex, shapeless and gelid, winking like frantic commas."

"Even Dad?" he said, crossing some curious line.

"You can't want me to tell you about your father as a lover, can you?" Cathleen asked.

Even the question was a terrible risk.

"My god, no!" he said. He did not, she was thankful, say yuk. "I meant it's hard to think of him as winking frantic."

What context spawned this disjunction? She thought this but did not ask. The mother she was likewise was his father's lover and their son knew so. He was not an idiot, he did have poetry courses. There was a poem to his father's scrotum sometimes anthologized which summons the image of a bullfrog's bloated and pebbly throat as the instance of that sack of flesh. In the poem the bloated throat became a drumhead and the hidden globes within it the eyelike innards of grapes.

The poem was popular among feminist scholars. The stone college where this day would end was famous for its feminists as well as its potters and harpists and historians. There was a chance Liam could find himself with someone—teacher or, worse, lover—who knew the frog-scrotum-drum-dark grape sequence. He would deny her thrice before his cock crows, she thought, laughing at the pun.

"Even beneath his black Lexus, your father, too, is sitting in the air," she said, ironic and solemn.

It was a statement about Noah as a lover as well, she knew, and she knew Liam would register a sense of it even without quite knowing. From his father, a lawyer, he inherited a sense of the justice of language and from his mother, the poet Cathleen Hogan Williams, a feeling that language makes you strong.

Noah's Lexus was an instance of women-and-boys. He had solemnly described its advantages to her as if attempting to convince her it was wise to purchase a car that cost what their house did when they first mortgaged it.

"The engine submerges in case of a front end crash, sliding under the passenger compartment rather than into it."

"Like ice blocks before the Titanic's prow," she had said.

"Come on, Katie," he said. It was the boy voice, not whiney, just almost hurt. He wanted her to hear him out. He was the solicitor and she the judge. She was to find him prudent.

"It can go from zero to sixty in six seconds and from sixty to zero in six seconds as well."

Twelve seconds of ecstasy, she did not say, and then you are still nowhere. Some people's sexual lives were so.

He lodged an objection against her silence.

"What are you thinking? You're laughing inside aren't you?"

He was hurt. He always wanted to know her insides.

"O sweetheart," she said, "it's a beautiful big car for a beautiful big lawyer and you can afford it and you like it so much. Why not do it then?"

He felt guilty. He wondered whether the money wouldn't be better spent if they put it away for Liam's college. He wanted to know what she was thinking when he asked about her silence.

"It's kind of a black hole, isn't it?" she said.

There was a confusion. His brow darkened, he thought she was saying the car was a suckhole in which all their energy would be spent. She was only half-thinking of something from long before. The collision of Volvos seemed to her something like the zero to sixty to zero. The truth was that in their day to day lives she almost never thought of Paul and when she did the memories were neither unpleasant nor hungry, neither shameful or saintly. More often she thought of his mother, whom she had met only once, denim skirted and strong, rocking in some room deep in the cool, wooden corridors of the house of cinnamon and cinnabar brick and dreaming of apples. Dead now, surely, not even a dry purse but dust and bird's skeleton.

"I mean it's a sort of experience that cancels itself, isn't it? Zero to sixty and sixty to zero, it's as if that moment never happened."

"It's a measure, Katie, not a moment. The safety margin."

"We are safest when nothing happens," she said. She kissed him and he let the summation drop. Within weeks he bought the Lexus and then prevailed on her to buy another, newer Volvo. She demurred. The Volvo was their first ever purchase as a marriage, before the house, it was twenty-one years old now, three years older than Liam, able to vote.

"What?" Noah asked. Sometimes jokes eluded him as he sat in the air, blocks of ice sliding beneath the prow of his floating fortress.

"The car has a vote," she teased. "It's twenty-one."

"It has a hundred and eighty-two thousand miles on it," Noah protested.

"A man in Africa drove his Volvo a million miles. I saw it on a commercial so it has to be real," Cathleen said.

"Do I have a vote?" Liam asked from the back seat of the Lexus.

"Are you twenty-one?" she asked. "No, but you do have individual comfort controls for your cabin temperature."

She sometimes thought Noah had purchased the Lexus because there was a database of the same name familiar to lawyers. Of the dream cars which traversed nothingness in twelve seconds she preferred the one named Infiniti.

Now Liam was sufficiently softened. She decided to try to mother him, just once more, in these last miles, these last hours.

"Can you say what was going on back there?" she asked him. "You seemed in an awful funk for a while."

He could say. He looked at her with a shocked affection, aware that she had cajoled him into talking, vaguely grateful.

"I don't know," he said, "it was like something just hung on to the car, some awful feeling. I was scared and angry."

Oh my dandy boy, she thought and did not say, my lovely dandy boy who can name his emotions like other men name the mountains.

"We are safest when nothing happens," she said.

"No one would want that," he said, getting the point exactly.

She told him a story about things that cling like dark clouds.

"Just below where we'll cross back over the river at Bear Mountain," she said, "is Dunderberg. Thunder mountain. Dutch sailors believed it was haunted by a goblin, such a perfect cliché of a goblin that you wouldn't buy it from Disney—all done up in stockings below a little tunic, a sugarloaf hat, and carrying a speaking trumpet, a sort of metal megaphone. This thing, the Heer of the Dunderberg by name, could order the winds around and whip up storms and fogs and mists full of sickness. It turned out that, if a ship didn't lower its topsail when it passed, the Heer would slip his little white hat over the mast and the ship would roll and tumble in the waves and thunder. Captains soon learned to pay it homage when they passed. They would dip their sails and nail a horseshoe to the mast as well, which may be where that whole thing started."

"Thanks, Mom!" he said, mocking, in the voice of a quiz show host.

"Passages are real," she said. "Passages are real is all," she repeated.

"I know," he said softly. "Thanks, really. It's just that—"

What? He couldn't finish. Just that I am scared, she thought, just that I do not know, just that I am becoming something I cannot yet imagine. I feel these fears too, she thought, for me they are also nameless. I, too, cannot say this. Unfinished his statement began to refute its fears and fill its possibilities. He dipped his sails and rode out a passage without a name.

Storm King, Eagle Valley, Crow Nest, Bear Mountain, Dunderberg.

Successions had their names and their stories.

"How do you still know so much now?" her son had asked her earlier this day.

She'd said she read the hills like memory. But she did not say she read her body like the hills.

Storm King, Eagle Valley, Crow Nest, Bear Mountain, Dunderberg downriver west. Beacon, Breakneck, Taurus, Fort Defiance, North Redoubt, Anthony's Nose, downriver east.

The truth was Paul had drilled her on the sequence and it had lain in memory nearly as long as Van Winkle had slept in nearby mountains.

It was a twenty year sleep ago they went together slowly over Storm King, crossed at Bear Mountain and reversed their track, stopping first in Cold Spring for coffee, and then going on to New Hamburg where she had first seen the mountain earlier in the summer and where he showed her an abandoned graveyard. There they made love a last, a second, time and slipped into each other's memories.

She lay in the arms of her lover only twice, once in a quilted heron's nest in an apple barn and a last time on the fern mound of a lady's lost grave.

Storm King, Eagle Valley, Crow Nest, Bear Mountain, Dunderberg. He so desperately wanted her to learn the sequence of the mountains it seemed as if they held a code for him. An encrypted poem perhaps:

> *O fairest flow'r*
> *no sooner blown than blasted*

"God, I know that sensation, that's good," Paul had said.

"Milton," she said. "A young girl's death. He was blind and remembered the briefness of what blooms."

"Apples blossom like white skirts and soon are edged with dust," he said.

"You said you didn't know poetry," she said and gripped his hand. (Now some twenty years after she could drive back not more than twenty miles and show her son the spot where she gripped her lover's hand on the dandy's cane of the pickup truck stick-shift. She could read the spot on the hills and remember where he rode her.)

"I don't," Paul had said. "It's a saying of Evelyn's—of my mother."

Cathleen felt the chill of age in an old woman's memories of a young girl's white skirts.

This, however, was the day of chicory. They kept time in blue.

It was past the time of apple blossoms, seasonably warm and along the margins of the road the dusty blue chicory.

There was a poem for chicory:

> chicory and daisies
> tied, released, seem hardly flowers alone
> but color and the movement—or the shape
> perhaps—of restlessness

"Is there a poem for everything?" Paul had asked her.

"Yes," she said.

"Storm King, Eagle Valley, Crow Nest, Bear Mountain, Dunderberg," he retorted.

"Teach me the names of apples," she said.

"Everyone knows the names of apples, mountains require us," he said.

It was an interesting usage: require us.

They knew she was leaving two days after.

After what.

"Donna mi Pregha," she asked him again to go out in the wide world with her, asked him to say *"in quella parte dove sta memoria?"*

Where is memory. What requires it of us.

"My apple is macoun," he said. "A melancholy sounding name for the sweetest of fruit, an apple of presence and texture."

"More?" she urged.

"Crow Nest singular, not apostrophe Crow's Nest, because they *do* nest there, nothing of the ship. For ships there is the Heer of Dunderberg..."

"And Eagle Valley?"

"They used to roost there and some say they have spotted them again in recent time, although the river is poisoned and their eggs grow too thin to sustain. You can still see red-tailed hawks rise up out of the river on an updraft and sail clear into Eagle Valley, disappearing up and back on outstretched wings without a single beat."

And will you go so, she thought, will I? Outstretched and without a single beat, the shape perhaps of restlessness.

She studied the light on the fair hairs along the curve of his earlobe. Who was he? What did memory require of us?

"Chicory," Paul said. "A perennial herb, *Cichorium intybus*, of the composite family, native to the Old World, widely natural-ized in North America, also called succory. Flavors coffee in New Orleans, best taken with beignet, sweet sugar doughnuts. There's a chicory cultivated for its edible leaves, known as radicchio, popular among the Italian tree men."

(We kept time in blue, she thinks twenty years after. Before yuppie time, in the time when radicchio had to be explained.)

"Chicory Macoun Radicchio," Cathleen had said. "Storm King, Eagle Valley, Crow Nest, Bear Mountain, Dunderberg."

She did not like what she had suddenly become for Liam during the last part of this drive, her chirpy font of earnest and secret knowledges most likely covering over a newly hatching grief, a wounded sparrow of pain stirring in the emptiness they gave the name of nest. The eggs grew too thin to sustain, the light of the world shone through, dimly opalescent, the vaguely caramel glow of light through stone at the Beinecke Library.

This was her soliloquy:

I am likewise afraid, perhaps more than you can know, as either son or husband. (It was a speech to them both she realized in a phrase.) I know this will surprise you both, for what you see of me is limb and angle, broad face, ample breast, saddened smile to be sure, but smile nonetheless. And stride. You see me stride and think I know the distance or at least the direction. Hips squared to the horizon, heliotropic, you'd make me the mother of morning, the wife of twilight if I let you. You think my poems incantations, something ballistic and with an inner track, and yet you also think them inadequate for what you face, despite you. You may be right in this, I feel it for myself. I know you will protest that they mean more to you than I can know and I do know this. But why you should think my poems any more adequate for our lives than I do is uncertain. I have been blessed to write poems in an age when poetry doesn't matter, when the purpose of poetry—as if such lofty phrases held anything—becomes itself uncertain. I suspect you would think I'd phrase this in terms of giving birth, although the truth is, if anything, it is more like making love and being made love to and with. Ridden in the double sense of the word, what's gone and what is upon one. I am sorry if this embarrasses you. The erotic crafts, I like the sound of that: sex, quilts, poems, pottery—yes, grafting apples—mothering. Does it surprise you that I would add a certain kind of driving to this list, that most manly of arts? How the hills give way and the tires sing as we try to understand the place of any one place in our lives, what it means to have lived in another time as someone else. Poetry is a car through darkening hills, where dusk comes early in recesses and hollows and where dawn illuminates distant peaks long before it settles back into these forgotten valleys.

She lost courage before she spoke it but it was no matter. She knew she would never have had the courage to speak it. The poem is what's left of all that is unsaid. It is like this good-bye we are living through together, my silent son and distant, worried husband. What's left to give before we give out?

The Heer of the Dunderberg sailed out on a transparent gust in a cloudless sky and draped their car with a grey parachute of melancholy. She heard him laughing through his speaking trumpet, a sound melodious and dark. She would have wept then for all she was losing but she did not want to hurt him any more than he was already.

What of Noah? This is not his story, except as they each think of him, and they do each think of him, both constantly and instantly.

MICHAEL JOYCE

What day is this? Saturday (she thinks, surprised, all time now blue and bound for stone, shrouded in a grey parachute), the old sabbath, he will worship things pastoral. (Do I make him sound foolish? she asks herself. He isn't. He is sweet and manifold as timothy grass, rich as clover, sturdy as blue fescue.) He will worship the pastoral either through golf, that awful game, or the yard itself, nosing the small green tractor around the ample thighs of oaks and the frailer birches, large foam earphones against the noise, sunshine's air controller, ground crew for the mother ship, so sweet in water-stained weejuns and sleeveless law school sweatshirt.

On the golf course he's an aerator, shoes spiked like the teeth of northern pike, white fringed flap over the instep. Lacoste pastel cotton. Still carries his clubs even among the ancient solicitors and barristers. Lettered as an undergraduate in both that awful game and lacrosse, both played with clubs. Sweet heart cave man.

Lost as anyone. His son gone. (O how she loves him!)

He tried to talk of losing Liam, not using those words, not "trying" in the sense of unable to talk. The man was a talker by profession, "Lady Justice's disk jockey," his phrase. And he had learned to talk in their marriage, she had taught him, and the truth be told—once he had gotten the hang of it, of talking from the heart—he had begun to teach her as well over the past decade.

She looked at Liam. Could he imagine that some things barely begin in the course of a decade?

She didn't ask him, didn't tell Liam the story of his father's bourbony night of sadness in a curious leather chair, a night that had begun with what could not be asked of fathers or told to sons.

She had been looking for Noah, it was a week ago or so, and could not find him in the likely places. Neither in the yard nor parked in the family room with Liam over soccer on the satellite television. They had a secret language of soccer between them, of pitches, kits and scowsers. Teams with names like Ajax (pronounced A-yaks, as if an exotic zoo) and Juventus (pronounced beginning with you). They knew the names and nicknames of a United Nations of players, identifying the latter by silhouette like world war two air raid wardens. Liam sat alone in darkness watching someone cook a fricassee on a cable channel. Noah wasn't there.

"Seen your father, Julian Child?" she asked.

"What?" he said. It was the so-weird voice.

"Your father Noah, the guy with the microbrews and channel changer."

"Ha ha ma, so hip," Liam flipped the channel. "I meant the Julian deal."

"Male for Julia Child," she said, "the doyenne of cable cooking."

"What?"

"The one with the funny voice."

Oh yeah, he knew. No father here. They had been talking and he wandered away. Bye.

Bye forever, she thought. Though I'll miss this mischief and sarcasm as much as the smell of baby powder. The smell of marijuana as well, she did not say.

Not in his study either. The black spoked wooden captain's

chair with the gold seal of the law school on its back. German chrome halogen postmodern desk lamp above the cherry wood desk. Tufted reading chair, a row of brass tacks like faceless gargoyles above this leather cathedral. Picture of her next to the chair. Liam likewise. Matching cherry frames.

The liquor cabinet was slightly ajar, unlike Noah and unlike Liam as well, who, when he stole from there, hyper-corrected, placing everything too precisely as it was.

She began to feel as if she were playing Clue. Mr. Mustard in the study with his cabinet ajar. He probably went for a walk, she thought.

But not without her. That was what they did on summer evenings, the two of them walking out among the wooded one-and-a-half acre plots of their largely unseen neighbors, on narrow lanes of carefully platted asphalt and carefully naturalized paths of cedar chips and pine needles. They walked out and looked for wildness—an occasional deer, a hawk, once—sweet god such a creature!—a fox, sleek and furtive as sex. And they walked out and looked for silence, the curls of autumn wood smoke from their neighbor's fireplaces giving way in the summer to barbecue smells of mesquite and hickory as well as the perfumed smoke from supermarket sacks of pricey wood chips—apple and cherry and piñon—for backyard smokers shaped like blast furnaces.

"Our neighbors would not know the shape of a blast furnace," said Noah once. "Only a working girl like you."

"Working girl means a prostitute," she explained to her husband the counselor. "Working class girl."

"Class," he said, "certainly."

"I could take up streetwalking if the tuition bills stack up," she said.

"Class," he repeated. "Poet and hooker Cathleen Hogan Williams."

No, he wouldn't walk without her. But he was nowhere.

She looked in the garage and found him in the car, burdened by something briefly bigger than himself and no space to consider it save the Lexus. The domestic history of places drove him there, the solid geometry with which he inhabited family room, study, yard, and suburban walkway didn't allow for an increase in the volume of worry.

He sat in the Lexus with a bottle of twelve-year-old bourbon, a thermos of ice, and a cut crystal whiskey glass.

She knocked politely on the window though she was aware that he knew she was there from the wedge of light the door had cut into the shadows when she opened it. He zipped down the silent electronic window and looked vaguely up at her.

"Sorry," he said. "Didn't mean to disappear."

"Just a sec," she said. She couldn't bear the sadness of his eyes and looped back to close off the wedge of light from the door. "Just what is branch water?" she asked, back at the car window and leaning over it like a girl in a drive-in root beer stand. "It's strange to get this age and realize I never really knew."

"Strange to get this age," he repeated. "Want a seat?" he asked and patted the passenger-side leather.

"I'd rather stand," she said. "It's a long flight."

"Liam asked a question I couldn't answer," Noah said.

"Hey, I'm not asking you to explain," she said. "You have rights. We all do. I wish you had a better space for it."

"I'm okay," he said. "I used to do this when I was a kid, maybe as old as this bourbon. Sit in the car in the garage and think."

"Of journeys?" she asked.

"I suppose," Noah said, "though I didn't know that then."

"He asks lots of questions I can't answer," Cathleen said, still leaning at the window.

Noah offered her the cut-crystal whiskey glass and she sipped. Smokey caramel essence and then a warm fire in the throat, the smoke fume lingering in the nostrils. We ought to drink more whiskey, she thought, perhaps when our son has gone.

"No," he said. "This one I can't answer for myself either. I mean there's lots of things he asks I don't know. Even things I realize I don't particularly care to know and yet don't blame him for asking. In fact wish him well in knowing. Even sometimes think if I had another life, or after this one, maybe I will see whether I still want to know them."

The bourbon had done a little work on his syntax and articulation. The words mouthed as slowly as the sentences formed. Enough to know what he meant though.

She waited. It was his to say or not what their son had asked him.

Noah looked up at her in the shadowy garage, his face like a moon, so sweet and sad she would have kissed it all over in some other time, a time of quarterbacks and root beer stands, a time of young lovers intense and newly married, a time of plump-breasted new mother and proud father in benchmade shoes. Now she looked on him with lonely love and hoped he felt its suffusion.

"It makes me angry and frustrated when I think that what

we are as individuals might not exist after death," Noah said.

These words were not as slow as the bourbon ones and in any case Noah's tone placed them in quotation. She knew Liam had spoken this to him. Not a question exactly, she thought, yet every question.

"There is a poet I love," Cathleen said. "You may remember my reading you her poem about the deer stuck in a subdivision or the one about her mother's fan. An Irish woman, Eavan Boland…"

Her words were not as deft as the ones she had greeted him with although her tone placed them in a rhythm they were used to between them. There was a poem for everything. She and Noah had made their marriage one.

He nodded yes. Asked the poem in silence.

"There's a poem in which she's walking back at dusk from a neighbor's house and feels herself disappearing…
I am definite
to start with
but the light is lessening
the hedge losing its detail
the path its edge."

"It's nice," he said.

It was not nice, she knew. She felt then what she felt now, that sense of glibness in the face of loss. No poems for some things, all poems inadequate for other things.

"What it was," Noah said from within the Lexus, "is that he already thinks some things that I do not recognize him in. I know he will think more of them. I know I want—we want—this for him. I just see him passing beyond."

She did not recite the way the poem marked such passing:

> *Suddenly I am not certain*
> *of the way I came*
> *or the way I will return,*
> *only that something*
> *which may be nothing*
> *more than darkness has begun*
> *softening the definitions of my body*

for it wasn't enough just now for the man in the leather seat and within this particular darkness.

"I'll be alright. I will," he said and patted her arm through the window.

"O I know that," she said. "We all will."

"Once," he said, suddenly making a speech, his own soliloquy, "during those two years Liam played baseball before soccer, a game went into extra innings and it began to get dark. Not dark enough to call it off but dark enough to make the outfield shimmer in a haze. The grass was like golden hay, the kids faces gold where the caps didn't shade them. I watched him chant the things they do in the outfield. He was in right, where they put the kids who couldn't catch all that well. I watched him chant that stuff they do: 'Hey batter. Come on Richie, pitch it in'— whatever the hell they say. The light came straight from the horizon and it was melancholy as hell, yet somehow happy. I got tears in my eyes watching him waiting there in the outfield."

When he said nothing more than this, she kissed his broad forehead, leaning way in through the darkness and the open window to do so.

"Don't stay out all night, love," she whispered. "He'll miss you. We both will. We love you."

"I'm not going to run the exhaust into the car or anything," he said.

Of course he wouldn't. Yet she recognized that he was self-conscious about how this scene had the qualities of mortal pageant. It was a scene of the sort they each hoped to avoid in their lives. A man seated in a car in a dark garage rhymed actual and emotional locales. The suburban comedy of deaths—not just unforeseen (weren't all deaths unforeseen for at least much of the lives of the dying ones? she thought), but unseen. The litany of losses, of garages, yards, and public spaces. Heart attacks over lawn mowers or center court, an ad exec with pancreatic cancer, soccer mom with a malign cyst half the size of a soccer ball, car wreck on the thruway swallowing up a neighbor's son and girlfriend, deer slug to an old man's temple. All this had happened within this gated enclave, the acre and a half of required buffer not half enough to stave off death.

There weren't words enough for this. Or rather there were words enough but no words were enough for this. There was a time when the aridness of everything she wrote appalled her, when none of it made sense, all of it like the annulling, coded language of the genome, a language made up of nothing but endless repetitions of A, T, C, and G, page upon page of these letters, as frightening as nonsense rhymes in an obsessive dream. Perhaps she felt that way still. Perhaps in some core of her beyond words nothing made sense, not the clasp of lover or son, nor that something which may be nothing, the night before us.

Not words enough to stave off death, she thought.

But this wasn't about death, she protested in vain to the white rectangle of the closed door. It was about life, a son going forth into the wide world and the second life they would have to form of their marriage. For a moment she considered going back into the garage to say this, but they each wrestled the same angel, she knew, and sometimes he required his moments alone. The dark angel's breath like violets, a damp draft his presence.

That was a week or so ago and now it was Saturday and Noah would be in the sunshine, the sweet smell of green grass all around him, calculating their progress against an inner almanac of the time-things-should-take, all thoughts of life and death behind him for a time.

Still perhaps it was hardest for him, she wondered, his son gone off, his wife away and no one to hold him.

Nonsense. No heart measures hope or loss more than another. Neither poet's nor advocate's. There was no hardest—no true marriage allowed of such comparison.

But could it be her way was hardest, not merely having to give up a boy however much she wanted to see him grow to this, but coming back to face a man who she never wanted to give up and who had no way to know how all this was, and had neither words to say it, nor eyes to see?

What if *she* could not speak it? What if she could not remember what she had seen among these hills? For the first time in a long time she considered the word infidelity.

What if words were never again enough, she thought. What if we are not enough for each other after this?

"Where's Dad?" Liam had asked that night when she came back from the garage.

"He's outside the house," she said, not wisely but exactly, "he has to work something out."

He nodded and went back to the his solitary fascinations. Their house seemed like a spaceship to her, the two men riding in flickering darkness, she moving through the shadows. It felt that way still.

Like that, death had entered briefly. It entered against the grain of growing expectation which began to fill the car as they crossed the modest bridge from Bear Mountain and headed toward Peekskill.

Liam was growing excited as their journey wound toward its end. What was that phrase he had stuck her with earlier as they were climbing toward Storm King?

Yes, he was fairly bouncing in his seat he was so excited. That was it.

And like that, deja vu, she recalled a grotto of death. Firemen in broad shouldered yellow slickers and curiously square helmets, like yellow samurai warriors, had stood before a smoldering car which gaped like a black cavity in the mouth of the mountain where the road from the bridge intersected Route 9D. She had forgotten it until this moment, until her recollection of Noah's dark night had left space enough in her reveries for death to settle in under the penumbral parachute which already shrouded the car.

The firemen poured water almost desultorily into the cinder of an automobile while two men in blue teeshirts and suspenders and tall black boots literally wrestled the angel of death with a medieval apparatus.

"The jaws of life," Paul had said, as if she should recognize the phrase.

They had known something was wrong when they came over the bridge. It was stop and go from the circle near the entry ramp with neither the time of day or the day itself offering any explanation.

"It must be an accident," Paul said, sitting up in the seat of the pickup truck and squinting as if it were possible to look beyond the traffic, bridge, and river.

"A car went off at Newburgh a year or so ago. It caught fire when it broke through the bridge rails and hit the water like a comet."

She began to cry then, long before they saw the car like a cinder.

"Please!" she moaned.

"I'm sorry," he said.

"Accident ahead," the man at the toll booth told them. "Careful," he said as though that was necessary.

They saw a car wreck on a sunny afternoon, the car a smoldering black cave that the firemen poured water into.

What she remembered was how little else there was. Just the rock cliff where the bridge met the mountain and the highway, the burnt car perfectly framed there, a row of blinking yellow fire engines bracketing either side of it in the sunlight. The traffic from the bridge moved through the throat of the mountain left or right in little stops like genuflections, a cop with a red baton waving them on, one by one, left upstream, right downstream. Two men in blue teeshirts pulled against a lever which turned a huge metal screw of gleaming silver steel as two desultory firemen poured water into the opening where they worked, soaking them.

Paul said, "There's still someone in it. In the wreckage."

"Stillborn," she remembered thinking. The wrong word. When it came their turn to stop before it and turn left, she could suddenly see that the firemen were not desultory at all. Their faces were in fact frantic. They poured water into the burnt black hole of the wrecked car as if it would bring the occupants back to life. The men in the blue teeshirts were also firemen, in yellow rubber pants but having shed their yellow coats to work the Torquemada device of the jaws of life.

No one would be born from this water. No one had come forth from this grotto.

"Promise me you won't ride in a car with anyone who's drunk or high," she suddenly said to Liam.

They were at the throat of the cliff where 9D went south and they with it. There was nothing there but the mountain and the road in sunlight. Still, she spoke this oath to him like a superstition, the way one crosses oneself seeing a black cat or a hearse.

She expected him to rail. He touched her sweetly on the cheek, the back of his hand curled like a fern soft against her.

"Not to worry, Katie Hogan," he said.

Sweet Jesus, she thought, the son assumes the father's sobriquets. She would have said something if she knew what to say. Maybe he hadn't really called her Katie, she considered.

"Promise?" she said.

"Promise," he said solemnly.

"You can have a promise a minute, Mom," he said. "Forty promises before we get there."

He knew the distance better than she did and she felt her heart fall.

Forty times forty minutes couldn't begin to fill the promises she held for him.

Like that, death had gone again, life drives off death to the margin of the field, where it lingers, in the shadow beyond the gold, not uninterested in what unfolds, not unmindful of the beauty of the boys who run across the space in lapsing sunlight.

It struck her then that perhaps Paul was dead by now.

She tried to recall where it was, not long before, that she thought she might see him along the highway.

He could be dead. She had already considered that Evelyn, his mother, surely was. Or perhaps not, flinty New England women lived on and on, she thought. A century no impediment for them.

It was New England here despite being New York.

She was thinking how much she liked that about this land-scape, the New England part of New York, yes, on the road down from Storm King when West Point seemed such a disappointment, where she thought how she didn't like the mountain's other shoulder, the thunder.

She recalled she had thought she might see Paul, her thoughts now looping in multiple orbits, the recollections of twenty years circling those of the last few hours. Forty minutes left.

Promise me you will always remember, promise me you will love and be loved, promise me there will be words enough, promise me you will live forever. O promise me the impossible, like any man, like any son.

Absurdly then, in the inner orbit of her recollections, she had thought what a delight it was to think that Washington and his men moved through these mountains: Beacon, Breakneck, Taurus, Fort Defiance, North Redoubt.

History was a comfort.

She laughed at the thought, but still, it was.

The fires moved from mountain to mountain, the British on the move. The same fires years later in celebration, leaping valleys like comet fire. One war over.

There was something which she could not tally in this, she who so hated death and war and the slaughter of young men, feeling—even then in the outer orbit, twenty years before—a swell of pleasure at the thought of these mountain men, taciturn and narrow of mien and buttock as Paul had been. There was a reality to them, simplicity of the time. She had felt it again, coming down toward West Point, crossing now from Bear Mountain toward Anthony's Nose.

The Virginia patrician, Washington, hadn't really ever trusted them. He couldn't wait when the war was over to recruit and train a proper professional army. He was full of complaints, Washington was, writing home to Martha from Newburgh about the dismal valley of the Hudson.

It was as likely a husband's tale, she thought. As likely a soldier's story.

He was afraid, she thought, alone and afraid like any man. That was the comfort history offered. We do continue.

"There's a lot of history around here," she said, a little too excitedly to Liam. He could hear it.

"Calm down, darlin'," he said.

Where was he getting these voices?

"Calm down yourself, Sundance!" she said.

He laughed, she laughed too. Sundance, where had that come from? They were both road loco and drunk with the future.

"Go for it, Miz Herodotus," he said. "Gimme a dose of local history!"

She swatted at him, implicated now in the craziness of what unwound before them, the end of something, the start of something.

She laughed and caught her breath.

Herodotus. God, the things your kids know without your knowing.

The story she liked was how Major Andre was caught. Paul had told it to her somewhere near here twenty years ago. He could be dead now, gone away to sea, a father himself again, a father twice or thrice over, his own sons gone or going. He could have gone to California and raised grapes in the Russian River valley. He could have learned to fly on wings of wax and feathers. He could live with his mother in a patterned brick house of cinnabar and cinnamon. He could have killed himself in an apple barn, hanging from the rafters in the sunlight. He could have made a killing as a radicchio farmer. He could live a century.

Forty minutes! Hardly time to remember the end of her story, hardly time to tell it, let alone tell the tale of Major Andre.

Promise me.

Nor had time stopped, she thought.

Already Liam's forty was thirty-seven, already the thirty-seven subtracted one as she spoke it. A stitch lost in the gleam of crochet needles.

This arithmetic she remembered from girlhood, how the minutes counted down to something and then opened up to something else. Ten, nine, eight, zero, one.

The ball descending upon Times Square and Guy Lombardo began another year of clear ice and January light. Meanwhile the New Year passed over the land like the shadow of an angel, Chicago and then Denver and San Francisco, the ball of light descending, another year lighting up.

The British ship lay south of him as he talked with Benedict Arnold and then, when it was fired upon by colonist militia, retreated still more downriver. He would have to make his way by land, a loyalist scout by his side leading him through the mountainous tangles, Fort Defiance and North Redoubt.

Major Andre was a hero because he was hung from a scaffold as an officer and died with dignity. So she believed, although she hated war. Benedict Arnold died on a British soldier's pension, hating the life he had chosen. So she believed, raised American Irish.

They were all sons of someone.

Thirty-three minutes and too many memories.

She and Paul had stopped once in Cold Spring for coffee, still a little railroad town along the river then, across from Storm King but not anywhere near the antiques bazaar it had become since. Still even then there were buttermilk scones to be had and Major Grey tea (in memory she almost slipped and thought Major Andre!) in a little guest house. She noticed Paul was morose, the pale innocence of his face clouded with some dark doubt. At the exact same instant the orphan form of a cloud's shadow, cumulus, sailed over Storm King like a zeppelin. It was very exciting for her, this synchronicity, as if life held instances of patterned enfolding like a paper Chinese fan.

Perhaps he loved her she thought.

Major Andre bid Benedict Arnold farewell and headed south to rendezvous with his ship, the loyalist guide leading him through moonlit paths and alders. Andre was disguised as a colonial, the plans for the West Point fortification tucked safely in his high officer's boots under homespun.

The guide was named Smith, she remembered. How?

"I might learn to play the zither," Liam said.

How could you? You can hardly play music on the radio. She did not say this, did not really believe it, though in jest—and silence—she thought it. Everyone had music, especially her son.

O promise!

Not zither but cello, she should have said, but she could not be certain that he had really said what she imagined.

If he loved her, Paul had not said so. Instead he wanted to talk the business of poetry. In view of the mountain, of Storm King, and over scones, he wanted to know what one did in the business of poetry. For him it was like apples. There was the blossom and the mystery to be sure, the fragrance of fruit and the color, but there were also markets and shippers and factors. Pesticides and graftings, Italian tree men, barn repairs, chimney flashing.

She was young then and thrilled to be published. She thought it was all apples and no trucks. Now she could tell him stories as ornate as Major Andre's. Of loyalists and rebels, ships anchoring downstream out of cannon's distance. Over these New England mountains in Cambridge, Providence and New Haven market prices were set, reputations were fixed. In the former New Amsterdam there were probably five people, three men and two women, who could make a poet's life as near a sinecure as it could ever get. They weighed and graded poems like apple factors; most consigned to supermarket bins, some few shipped to the boutique fruit shops like museum pieces or to far-off Japan as objects of veneration.

The souls of apples, the weight of poems.

Twenty-six minutes and as many promises.

In her mind she used to mix it up and think that it was his shiny officer's boots that did in Major Andre. Even now when she had the story straight she still liked to remember it so. The Loyalist guide Smith turned back for some reason, never explained in the stories, neither the one Paul told nor the ones she'd read since. In a poem she imagined it was for his wife and family that Citizen Smith turned back. He had a new child and could not be about all night, he had a premonition. In any case Smith left Andre to his own devices, not far from safe territory and the river where the British ship waited. Before long the weary Andre broke through into a clearing and friendly faces.

This was her favorite part of the story. She could remember Paul's face as he told it, clear and firm as French-milled soap, ruddy, rosy cheeks and hard, strong hands with round knuckles like crab apples, fair hairs along the curve of the earlobe. Looping in multiple orbits, the visions of twenty years circling those of the last few hours.

Twenty-five minutes left.

I used to be a ballerina and I rode a silver horse. Promise.

The two men in the clearing would have looked like Paul, she thought, that bright and canny innocence, a laconic reserve, wary but friendly enough. The British Major would have made them out as primitives, not different from Smith, homespun and blue-eyed and brave as foxes.

The crumbs of scones littered the linen table cloth and she picked them up with her finger tip and conveyed them to her lips, sweet soft crumbs. Storm King rose opposite, green as an apple, the half globe of it scored with the road they had just come over, all life ahead of her, Major Andre's shiny boots giving him away.

"Do you have that sheet with the map and the schedule?" Liam asked.

It was the tone that blamed her and which on any other day she would have handed back to him. It was not her place to live his life or keep his things—CDs, soccer flats, teeshirts, concert tickets, college orientation sheets, crimson-colored condoms in pretty foil wrappers—in place.

"You do," she said gently, reaching to touch him with the soft back of her hand ."Don't worry, love, there'll be signs and guides everywhere and kids and parents who've lost their maps, their wits, their breakfasts, and god knows what else this day."

"How do you know about Herodotus?" she asked.

"What?" he said, half protesting, then minding his behavior.

Lots of time had passed since saying that and he only half remembered.

Actually sixteen minutes had passed, twenty-four remaining.

"I learned it in gym class," he said, eyes sparkling.

She laughed aloud.

"It wasn't his boots that did him in," she said, "though they shone in the moonlight. Major Andre had mistaken their faces for Tories and identified himself as a British officer. It's an exemplary tale, really, how the English misread the faces of the new nation, unable to tell that, even though these new trees were grafted upon the same stock, they gave forth rebel fruit."

Liam allowed her to say all this without protest, though she was certain she had not recited the preliminary story aloud. He was making allowances with the oaths and promises of the passing minutes.

"And they searched his boots and found the plans and he was hung as a spy," Liam said. "We did learn that in History."

"When Benedict Arnold got the news he bid his wife goodbye and went down from West Point to the Hudson where a fast barge waited to take him to what they thought would be battle or a meeting of officers at some remote station. Instead he ordered them downriver and to the ship that awaited the captured Major Andre."

The zeppelin of shadow passed over Storm King. Paul's sweet, native face resumed a patrician reserve. Scones done, tea leaves settled in the small pot. They resumed their course upriver and to the end of summer and someone else. Twenty-two minutes left.

Sometimes when they made love Noah whispered that he wished he could once be able to see someone else make love to her. It wasn't anything kinky, she thought, or no more kinky than what they allowed themselves in fantasy and reverie. He merely wanted to witness what he felt, see the face of ecstasy.

He was a man of witness.

Still, she couldn't help sometimes thinking he might feel something of the past in her embrace, some distant and untold otherness.

Only five human lovers in her whole life, like stone beads. Four men, a girl she had loved once in college. Quite literally (though hungrily) once, a sweet night, tangerines in bedsheets which smelled of chlorine bleach, the sweeter taste of each other, a delicate and reticent morning farewell. Occasionally seeing one another on campus and at meetings of the literary quarterly.

O and two hundred poems at least, also lovers. Though the poem of Major Andre incomplete, never right, never published. Shiny black boots in the moonlight under homespun, mountains scored like apples.

Sometimes she considered the sadness of Benedict Arnold's wife.

"Do you think we should call Dad and tell him that we got here okay?" Liam asked when they were ten minutes away.

"Well we didn't yet really, did we?" she said lightly. "Let's call him when you're settled."

"I guess you're right," he said.

Noah's cell phone was still somewhere there under the mess of stuff in the back. She had promised Noah she would take it, even though Liam had his with him, even though she detested these things that carried their own spaces with them, unfolding within the silence like a tent of noise.

"We are only going downstate," she said, "not down the Zambesi."

It was a figure from childhood movies, the Zambesi, river of mystery.

"Please?" Noah had asked. "For me?"

"For you I will take survival rations," she said, nuzzling him, "beef jerky and tricolor freeze-dried Neopolitan astronaut ice cream."

"Be sure to call me on the cell phone when you eat that hyphenated ice cream," he said.

Funny man.

And a man connected to things by as many umbilicals as an electronic spider, she thought, the metaphor mixed as horribly as electronic life itself: fax and cellular phone, beeper and infra-red modem. Even the keys of his Lexus sent off alien beams which could set the thing to blinking and honking like a black-and-white kids' cartoon from her childhood. Leapin' lizards Annie, it's Steamboat Willie's Stanley Steamer!

Ever his father's son, Liam had jammed and crammed the back of the Volvo with things electronic: gameboy, game system, powerbook and powerbar, television and telephone, fan and cube-sized refrigerator, microwave and shortwave, several hundred CDs at least, as many books, software and game cartridges, CDROM and videotape, twenty or more teeshirts with the faces of obscure British rock stars, an actual Robert Mapplethorpe print of a photo of a naked woman.

Now these objects hung over her like an avalanche, the comet's tail of detritus along the crest of a storm-born wave on a windy beach.

Not more than five minutes. Wind, beach, comet, avalanche, we enter the land of mixed metaphor, she thought. My boy almost a man, my car full of his childhood and about to tumble into the black hole which transforms childish things to leather upholstered opinions and chrome consciousness.

O she meant neither to malign her husband's vehicle nor his person nor her son's future in this half-curse. But damn them for what they took from her, for what she would have given them (did give them) without their asking.

In the traffic around them other college-bound families likewise slipped just ahead of the avalanche. She met the eyes of other mothers, some of them chromed to be sure, but most like her uncertain of what would become of what they had given birth to.

Damning and loving at once. Legs spread once and then once again, now this giving without asking.

Sister eyes, surprised.

It was the time of easy rhymes as well, the satisfactions of wordplay.

In the outer orbit, in the time outside of time, they came finally, she and Paul, through Beacon and Hughsonville and then left toward the river into New Hamburg, retracing the first steps of her summer at its end.

It wasn't a town he was fond of, though he liked the estuary of Wappinger's Creek and the ridge of trees along both sides which made it seem a canyon.

There was a blue heron in the shallows. A bird of synchronicity.

The creek pooled out and met the river as the road descended into New Hamburg. Just then however Paul had detoured up along a rise which forked off left and back uphill paralleling the river.

There was a monastery he wanted her to see.

"It's you who is the monk, not me," she said. "You should wear the sandals in the family."

He looked at her with spooked amusement, the twinkle of fables in his eyes.

"I was once here," he said and she had strained to hear where the punctuation had fallen in the sentence he spoke.

"You were a monk?" she laughed despite her.

He pinked with embarrassment.

"Yes, it's funny."

"When?"

"Post high school and post growing up with the countesses, pre-Cornell, pre-wife and pre-Italian hermitess, in the days of Italian tree men."

"Jesus," she said, likewise a funny thing to say.

"I was, and am High Church, a protestant, you know," he said. "There wasn't any issue about it then for several reasons. The world had recently become ecumenical and I didn't intend to become a priest and, most important, Evelyn was able to pay the full dower for a brother's portion."

"And your father?" she asked. It was the absolute first word she had spoken of his father.

"Still dead. Dead before then. Dead almost always," he said these words like a chant, past bitter but not comic. A rhythm she knew. Even then as all her life and more and more even now,

~169~

Cathleen was careful never to say sorry when someone disclosed a death. It had seemed to her from sometime in her adolescence that you shouldn't say sorry about death since it was so constant. It would be like saying sorry at the rain.

"It must have been very hard for you," she said.

They had reached a stone wall along a narrow road through tall green trees and lush hedges. There was a single steel rail across a gap in the stone wall, the rail propped up on a lip of stone on either side of the gap. He lifted it off and like that they were in an orchard, high above the Hudson. Beyond them tall black walnut trees traced a dark canopy of shade around the mustard stone of the monastery.

There in the blue haze downriver beyond the Newburgh bridge like an emerald hay mound was Storm King.

"O king of kings," she whispered.

"So we chanted then and now," said Paul.

"And an orchard," she said. "You must have thought you were in heaven."

"It was a draw," he conceded. "For me and them I suppose. Brother Appleman."

"Were you given—?" she asked. He had! She could see in his eyes, the secret, the same pink of embarrassment as earlier. He had been given a name in the monastery!

"Will you tell me?" she asked.

"I'll whisper it sometime," he flirted.

"Whisper now," she flirted back, reaching to touch his smooth chest through the buttons of his short-sleeved shirt.

There had been something erotic about the monastery orchard overlooking the downriver highlands.

"It was why I left here," he said in a teasing voice, twisting away. "At eighteen years old you begin to see naked nymphs on treetops in the sunset. Apples hang like soft breasts, a cleft in the stone wall gives you a hard-on. *Domine, non sum dignus:* it wasn't the life for me."

He touched the tip of her nose with a teasing finger, soft, inviting.

"There are other secret places near here," he said.

"Tell me," she begged, softly.

"Brother Maria Charles," he whispered, fixing her eyes in his.

"Maria Carlo," he corrected. "They are an Italian order, *mi fratelli.* Another sort of tree men…"

He didn't particularly like New Hamburg. How wrong he was, she thought.

"The town seems a second thought, down there," he said.

Actually it was. A late nineteenth-century village of German railway men's bungalows where in other years there had been a smelter and a rendering plant and a steamboat stop and a boatyard and years before that ice racers along the river.

She liked the thought of ice racers, sliding out in long strokes like Hans Brinker, a stride ahead of winter. These, however, were sailboats with iron sled rails under them.

"Sixty miles an hour from here to Poughkeepsie, sometimes a racer would tumble off and be sliced in half."

Cathleen winced and he said he was sorry, as if apologizing to the rain. She thought of the loop of water which couldn't soften the gape of death at Bear Mountain earlier. She thought of the stain of blood blazed across long gone ice.

"There were scheduled Hudson sloops out of New Ham-

burg in the glory days," he said, "but I don't know whether there
were whalers."

"Whalers?" She caught her breath.

"Oh yes," he said. "There were whalers up and down, as far as
Hudson, New York. A Poughkeepsie sailor wrote a tale of ship-
wreck in the South Pacific. He was kept in a wooden cage by
pygmy cannibals, like Gulliver, and lived to tell about it."

O the world's a series of stories, she thought, a gap in the
wall, windows in windows, everything linked, the whole ball
strung with unnoticed silk. Sometimes the morning star was
caught in an apple barn's high window, other times fireflies
turned the world's riggings to shimmering chains of light.

The truest saints saw nymphs in treetops, she thought, and
the whole universe kept them erect.

The blue heron was gone, replaced by five swimming swans.

The world was windows in windows and in some other story
time was up while in this one it had merely begun to open.

He had one more secret place to show her here. Halfway
down the hill toward New Hamburg, past the bridge over the
estuary but not yet to the crossroads which went down to the
railroad, he stopped opposite an ugly chain-link fence shrouded
in an oily tarp which masked a sunken oil tank sitting on a
cinder rise just above the sunbaked tracks. It was a place where
trucks filled up with heating oil.

"We'll park here," he said and then they hiked opposite, up
through the heat into the hill rather than down through the
cinders toward town and the river. It hardly seemed a trail where
they went in, more a cleft in thin trees along a steep hill, some of
the tree trunks wreathed with poison ivy.

There was nonetheless a path beneath, occasionally grinning like a fresh scar, elsewhere crisscrossed with berry brambles like barbed wire.

"Careful," he said but the brambles striped her legs, a drop of dark crimson descending slowly to her ankle like a miniature blood sunset.

The path rose in a series of gentle switchbacks, not more than two hundred yards vertically, a lazy Z upward, the last fifty yards through huge ferns, their leafy fronds the size of faces, to an abandoned graveyard.

It was a peaceful and fantastic landscape, shaded ferns and fallen gravestones like books made of bone. John Orchard buried improbably next to Mary Hambly, Jane Bloom within reach.

Cathleen was speechless.

At last we come to this, she thought, lapsed stones gently nestled in greenery above a distant river, the peace of bees and monarch butterflies moving among poplar trees. At one time pallbearers had swayed beneath the weight of caskets up along the switchbacks of the path.

Paul led her silently on the part of the path that circled the graveyard to where it looked down on the opposite side of the estuary and beyond toward the highlands. Both waterways were obscured now by the lushness late in a deciduous summer, though fall and spring must surely open the window again, she thought, disclosing the river and the broad water of the creek which fed it and the mountains beyond.

She turned back toward the graveyard, which now looked like a green jaw with flat and broken teeth.

"How?" she asked in a whisper.

"A congregation dwindles or turns poor, children move away and old people die off. A thousand things," said Brother Maria Charles.

"But," she protests, "the history—"

"Most of the stones are nineteenth century, a few here and there eighteenth, the half dozen or so Dutch graves worn away to nothing, though they had some rubbings from years ago at the monastery. There's lots of history around here," he said.

And the catacombs of Paris are stacked crisscross with a geometry of a million bones, she thought, skulls woven like rickrack into beaded walls, zigzag patterns of intervening lightning. The bones of Hindi dead float in saffron pyres upon flaming rafts to the sound of bells. In the cliffs near here fifteen thousand years ago the first people scratched petroglyphs and buried their dead shrouded with woven grass in thin graves.

All gone, these at least remaining.

Life seemed something to grab.

She clung to him then and took him in a rush, sinking him with her into the cool and mounded soil within the ring of stones. What started swiftly ended holy and slow. It was, she thought in retrospect, the most passion she had felt in her whole life and, though never lost, in some sense lavished on a stranger, on a forgotten grave, in a place without a name above a river.

He whimpered at her embrace, she remembered. She was a large woman and he was fair and slender and she pulled hard against him, her fingers drawing blood as she scratched into his buttocks. Yet the whimper was for so much else, she knew. Things lost. Things still dead and dead before then. Things passing.

Not long after she would go back to her husband and their

plans of children. Not long after she would have one son, not long after that none more. Not long after her son would go away. Soon perhaps he, too, would have sons or daughters. Perhaps Brother Maria Charles was dead, perhaps he lived happily ever after.

She had turned away from him when they were spent and sat facing outward, her heels drawn up modestly before her, slowly buttoning the skirt and bodice of the long linen shift. With each button she parsed the declensions of passion.

Loved, loved love, will love, love; having loved, having been loved, will have been loved, loving.

They stood and finished their toilet back to back, chaste as puritans. She was not Heloise but Hester. He was, beneath the flint, her Italian summer.

Maria Carlo Caro Mia.

They faced each other clothed in the innocence of Adam and Eve, smiled, or so she remembered.

Stories end in any orbit.

She had felt, she swore, the rush of some spirit, a dark liquid up through her spine and temples, turning to sparks and stars and screaming as she reached orgasm, her feet straining, toes dug and heels upward, a scent of loam and distant honeysuckle, sun through the trees suddenly blinding, and then the slim creature gone.

The place where they stood—where they had lain—was near a grave whose stone was cleft in both its upper left and lower right quarters, its letters worn to grainy shadows, mostly readable:

MICHAEL JOYCE

Hester
daughter of Daniel and Harriet
Van Anden
June 15. 1862
Aged 20 years
and 19 days
The months of affliction are over
the days and nights of distress
We see her in anguish no more
She has found a happy _____

Hester. It was the truth, however coincidental, the way the story goes. The letters were curlicue and vaguely italic.

"The S is like the sharp cleft," she said to Paul.

"Clef," he reminded her.

So it was. Key not crevice, she thought, the wrong word.

Cathleen tried to parse the empty space where the stone was worn away at the line's end. It was a difficult scansion, not at all clear where or whether the rhyme would fall. She tried a series of words and rejected each in turn.

> space
> share
> peace
> bower

She rubbed her fingers over the dim word, squinting to bring the worn letters into focus.

Such a young girl, twenty years and nineteen days.

A young girl herself then, twenty-seven.

As they began to leave she looked once more and suddenly

saw, as clear as anything, that the last word must be "release."

She felt vaguely disappointed at this word. The irony of it annoyed her and in any case it was awkward, release no redemption for a young girl's nights of anguish. Cathleen wished her sister Hester Van Anden a better share. She would rather that the girl had found a happy bower than mere release after so short a life and an uneasy verse.

Downhill she avoided the brambles, going way around through whip saplings and back to the trail over unsteady stones. Even so, her ankles were raw with the stripes where the thorns had cut her on the way up Reese's Hill.

For Reese's Hill, he told her, was its name, though he didn't know what the graveyard had been called or the name of the lost congregation. He also told her how she could take the sting from the scratches on her ankles with a compress of chamomile. He recommended soaking a tea bag and applying that. It might surprise her to know, he said, that an equally soothing balm could be made by steeping nettle flowers in season. They talked easily enough on the way back upriver, though softly and at intervals, each of them knowing what was over and what had been. They had learned to name some things and they had considered—both separately and aloud—divers ways to relieve afflictions. Back up the Hudson they bid each other farewell and, however unhappily, saw each other never after.

Now in memory their passion, as all passions, seemed dearly purchased. She longed for what was lost, not just the lover and his flinty mother, but Hester Van Anden and the unknown others above whose bones the earth had boiled like a fatty soup, she riding the froth, longing also for her own mother and The

Tennessee Waltz, for her lost daughters and her momentarily present, soon to be gone son.

She had worried how they would unload the weight of Liam's life into this new place and even considered hiring a day worker, a porter from a temp agency, in some parody of nineteenth-century gentry.

Instead, the college was teeming with healthy children in bandanas and welcome buttons, upperclassmen dispatched to greet the arriving freshmen, or whatever they called fresh and upper in these new days her son would enter. There were handsome tanned boys with weightlifter muscles, soccer shorts, and ready smiles, and round-breasted girls in leotards and tight little shorts called bun-huggers, nipples blossoming through the elastic fabric like moly flowers.

Someone served her lemonade with mint in a real glass of ice.

Everything was looked after and at.

The girl who brought her lemonade slung an arm around her waist and embraced her like a daughter. They were watching Liam manfully waltz a box much too large for him into the dormitory just ahead of one of the muscled boys from the welcoming committee. "He'll be fine," the lemonade girl said. "He seems really cool for a freshman. Very intense." They were judging him, his mother and a stranger. Some day another stranger would hug her, his wife if they still had wives then.

The girl squeezed her once more and then she too went to carry Liam's things from their Volvo to his room. Everyone has seen where he will be but me, thought Cathleen, feeling temporarily unnecessary. She drank the dregs of lemonade, chewing on the mint leaf. Placing the glass precariously on a stone pilaster, she grabbed a box for herself, a pristine cardboard carton with cutout handles which Noah had purchased for this purpose from a moving company. "Desk things," Noah had written absurdly in block letters with a black magic marker.

Liam went somewhere scheduled while similarly scheduled she joined other parents in the college chapel where they were congratulated by the president, a silver-haired and handsome man in a linen suit, for raising such thoughtful men and women. How he knew this she could not say. Nor she suspected, could he. Afterward there was champagne in an herb garden with trays of speared fruit and cubes of conventional cheese. The president shook sundry hands though she did not give him hers.

After an hour she and Liam met up as planned and made a trip back into town on the pretense of picking up a few things he had forgotten, shampoo and a clock, peppermint toothpaste from Maine, a half dozen other toiletries and a desk lamp, which nonetheless added up to something under sixty dollars.

She pressed the change from a hundred dollar bill upon him together with another fifty. He resisted.

"Think, Mom, can you imagine how much cash Dad attempted to give me?"

She imagined. Stories ended. There was little else to say or do as they drove back to his campus. She had the absurd but uneasy feeling that she had been supposed to leave once the silver-headed president congratulated her and fed her champagne and fruit. She was relieved to see other parents likewise still knocking about, smiling awkwardly and looking equally frightened and out of place.

Who would they give themselves to now? she wondered. Not that they had given themselves solely to Liam or, for that matter, at all—not any more than a stone gives itself to the swell or the skin its dander to air. We have diminished and grown, she thought, and it would be absurd to think that our marriage depended on its offspring.

He was that now, sprung off, not gone. "Go, dumb-born book," she recalled the invocation of a poet long gone. Sprung off, a dumb-born boy in the lost, now newly incorrect sense of that word, speechless, a tongue at first fit only for song. Where had he learned the words he knew now? What words next?

Why then could these words not stave off the growing panic about their meaninglessness that she felt among these doe-eyed, dumb-born ladies. Not just the ladies meaningless but she and her mate and the words that named them all. What would be absurd would be to occupy a cliché more intimately than a vow. Empty nest could serve either the dry, careful basket of the robin fallen from a frond or the muck spot of the long-ago heron.

Launching him they launched themselves again. Was witherward a word? They could not count on the shore (nor, she thought, was shoreward necessarily right for a marriage, which should flow, should flow).

Liam lingered by the steps of his new dormitory. He was eager to be up there, where his life was, but sweetly waited for her to say what she had to say, kiss him, and bid him good-bye.

"I'll call," she said.

"Don't—" he said, then amended. "Don't forget we go away to some goofy camping trip to get to know each other. It will probably be better if I call you in a day or two."

"Probably," she said.

She hugged him again. Then once more. "This one for your father," she whispered into his hair. "I promised him I would."

"Hug him back for me."

Liam's eyes were moist. She should go now though she suddenly wanted to tell him so much, suddenly wanted to relive the whole twenty-year journey again.

Where is our story? she thought. Perhaps we are cleansed of it at intervals. What we were was see-through, what we are is unshaped and ahead of us. The spine of any definition removed from us in the way one slips the transparent quill from within the milky tube of a cleaned squid. The transparent quill writes with invisible ink, viscous as the gleam snails leave in a garden under the moon. Falling star, lover's touch, mink's eye, worm burrow—all gone by morning.

Though linked, her stories and Liam's now were severed, each of them alike now occupying spaces of gaining differences, no matter that the automobile seemed to her familiar and the musk scent of his cologne still lingered there. In some sense he birthed her in this stone hut he retreated to. Each of their clocks ran forward and back in different orbits, the numbers spinning so fast they couldn't be read, merging into a blur like blasted roses or that place at the universe's end, seen through the Hubble telescope, where molten stars are born.

This arithmetic she remembered from his birth, how the minutes counted down to something and then opened up to something else. Ten, nine, eight, zero, one.

And so, opening to infinity, her son's childhood ended, or at least some portion of it—though not as much yet, she thought,

MICHAEL JOYCE

as he might imagine. He had turned and waved once more, inclining his head toward her like a puppy, his eyes glazed with increasing excitement, wishing her love and gratitude and gone. And gone she was.

It was a curiosity to her that you could give up memories and yet in the giving retain. If only she were a better poet she could account for, if not explain, this paradox.

She was a little afraid of the emptiness before her and all the names for it. The light was lapsing, the summer already gone into autumn, at least at day's end. She would not take the mountain route home but instead would make her way again along the opposite bank without stopping for the night. She would call Noah sometime, but, although she longed for him she wanted now to be alone, if only to confirm that she always ever was alone, each of them so given to the wide world her son now, too, moved through on his own.

CHAPTER SIX

A Meteor Shower

Cathleen beeped him not long after he and Antoinette reached the screen house. There was no phone there and so he had to go back up to the house.

"Are you alright?" he asked Antoinette.

"I'm fine, go to your wife," she said.

"Are you alright?" he asked Cathleen when he reached her on the phone.

"Alright but more weary suddenly than I can imagine. I'm sorry, Noah, I'm going to pull in for the night. I'll leave at dawn, I promise, I'll be there with you before the light."

"Stay somewhere—"

"I'll stay somewhere nice," she anticipated him, "promise. A place with chintz and little reproductions of impressionist paintings under glass."

"That's pheasants," he said.

"What?"

"Pheasants under glass."

She laughed.

She had almost hung up without asking about him. It was the only clue he had that she was more upset than she seemed. He told her where he was and what he was doing.

"How sweet," she said. "She must have known you needed someone now."

I need you he wanted to say.

"I love you," she said. "I'm glad you have a girlfriend."

It shocked him.

"Don't kid about it," he said.

"I'm sorry," she said. "I'm glad you're there with her, Noah, it makes it easier for me to stop. Sometimes things happen for a reason."

"Very poetic," he said. "No wonder you're famous."

"Fuck famous," she said.

"There's that," he said and sighed.

"Before the light, I promise," she said.

He missed her. He had hung up without telling her his discovery about the French woman.

He knew well the procession past weariness to dawn, staying up through the night, moving past midnight beyond the lagging, empty center of the dark and then onward toward the hours of promise when morning seems as likely a destination as either sleep or dream.

Even so, and not counting the short, sleepless nights or false dawns of occasional flights to Europe, it had been longer than he could remember since he last stayed up all night. He had forgotten how lovely it was to sit awake and keep vigil beside a sleeper, the light on the fair hairs along the curve of her earlobe, the smell of her sleeping like the smell of a mountain or the moon, alien spaces despite what little he knew of their names or phases.

He hadn't been surprised when Antoinette Ryan slept in the

boat but he was rather relieved that he felt no temptation to sail off there himself.

"Well, there's Nod after all," he whispered when he saw her fold down across the narrow bench of the guide boat with her head against the gunwale.

"Very nice, Mr. Williams—" she muttered, then corrected herself in a yawn. "Very nice Noah…" as used to moving silently in and out of sleep it seemed as she was to moving silently through space.

He rowed silently in, the dip of oars making arcs in the still surface of the night.

"We have Wynken and Blynken but there's no Nod," she had said to him hours before when they set off from the small dock in the old Adirondack guideboat which she had convinced him to untarp and slide down from beneath the screen house and across the tall grass to the shore.

The boat had been unexpectedly light to move, its prow carving a notch through the grass deep enough to capture though not hold the milky light of a sliver moon which set not long after.

Noah knew the nursery rhyme from when Liam was young but he thought it came from Mother Goose.

"Oh no," she said. "It was Eugene Field, the poet of childhood as they called him, perhaps better known to you for Little Boy Blue than for the Dutch lullaby."

She recited with the singsong charm of a schoolgirl, pulling the shawl up around her shoulders and head, then holding her hands out before her at her hips in a gesture of declamation:

Wynken, Blynken, and Nod one night
  Sailed off in a wooden shoe
Sailed on a river of crystal light,
  Into a sea of dew.
"Where are you going, and what do you wish?"
  The old moon asked the three.
"We have come to fish for the herring fish
  That live in this beautiful sea."

Noah applauded, the echo of it slapping across the stillness of the water and setting off the bullfrogs and then the loons.

"And where are you going, and what do you wish?" she asked.

"Which am I?" he asked.

"Blynken, I'm certain," she said.

"I wish I knew how you got me into this," he said. "Or for that matter how I'll get you into that little boat."

"I'll get me in if you get you in first and steady it," she said.

It had been surprising how easily she skipped into the boat— "Don't you dare utter the word spry!" she admonished him— how light she felt when he took her hands to help her in.

"You can have your Cezanne," she said. "This boat is our masterpiece! It's fitted out in cherry wood and was built just about the time we came over here in quite a different kind of boat, my brother and I."

"Keep saying that and I'll take it," Noah teased.

"I wish you would, Mr. Williams," she said, "I wish you would, better you than some museum that will store it in a corner, better you than selling it in some awful auction."

"The moment I lift the painting from you they would lift my

license for malfeasance," he said. "We can talk on other days about some options you might have."

"Yes counselor," she said again in that way she had of teasing him with the term.

So be it. It was what he was he thought. He counseled, gave forth conventional wisdom like a map does, careful of the terrain, conservative, observant of the poles, uncolored by mere circumstance.

She settled into the wicker seat amidships or whatever you called the center of such a boat. Then she recited again.

"Of the Adirondack guideboat one Mr. Henry van Dyke at the turn of the last century said, 'they are one of the finest things that the skill of man has ever produced under the inspiration of the wilderness. It is a frail shell, so light that a guide can carry it with ease, but so dexterously fashioned that it rides the heaviest waves like a duck and slips through the water as if by magic.'"

She had spoken the words as truly as a map, so much by rote that he thought at first she was reading from something, a little crib sheet she kept under the wicker seat or pasted to the thwart.

"My brother Brian loved this little boat, god rest his soul."

They had lived here as brother and sister beginning after first his wife and then her husband died and before he too died and Antoinette went away to the coast of the sun.

"I don't know how you do that," Noah said, "how you recite those things at your age."

"My age indeed!" she said. "It's not a matter of age at all. Some are trained to memory and others to quickness."

"Me?" he asked.

"Neither, counselor," she lifted water from the lake in her palm, let it pour back again. "Some are given to a middle way. My brother was like that also, given less to memory than action, more to memory than passion. It's the middle course and it gets you through the straits."

Her voice had turned briefly melancholy, these recollections were another side of the Brian she had told him about.

"Please," she said, lifting her hand from the water and indicating the gape of the dark lake. "You do the honors, counselor, let's set off..."

For ten years, from nineteen until the great crash of nineteen twenty-nine, Brian Mulvey had saved every penny which came into his bootblacked or callused hands, short of what he needed to feed and clothe his sister and him and keep a roof over them, the latter not difficult things to do cheaply enough, all things considered, in the hotel trade.

Consider thirty-six hundred and fifty days plus a day or two for leap years, less the five-day bout of scarlet fever which scarred his heart and many years later eventually killed him, minus, five years into it at age seventeen, two days to get married and, four years after that, three days to wake his wife and bury her together with all his hopes for family. Figure, conservatively, one dollar a day banked for the first two years as a bootblack, increasing to, let us say, three and a half dollars for the next five years at two jobs, at Crotty's hotel by day as doorman, then clerk, then eventually manager, and by night at the smelting plant until Crotty found him out and thereafter at the Crotty warehouse where he put the boy on second shift or third when the hotel needed him for both the first and second. Compound it. Compound it again and again. Meanwhile take the contents of their auntie's satchel and add in another stack of cash which Antoinette suspected was from gambling and you had the grub-stake for a very successful business as the maker and shipper of bootleg whiskey. Compound it all again for three years before the crash where he somehow managed to lose almost nothing in bank failure.

"Didn't he ever feel guilty about taking the money from the satchel?" Noah had asked.

"You and your satchel," she said. "Is that all you can think of? Guilty how?"

"It belonged to the policemen who sent it to their mother."

"Did it?" she asked. "It belonged to whom they sent it to, the whole line of women who pulled lambs out of bloody hills!"

"It belonged to you then," he said.

"It came to me then, didn't it?" she said, smiling.

When the market crashed Crotty crashed with it, and a man with cash in hand was—"if he looked sharp and played his cards right, and the Holy Mother knows Brian Mulvey looked sharp," she said—sitting pretty. He bought Crotty's hotel and Crotty's warehouse, then someone else's hotel and someone else's again.

"He only needed the one warehouse," Antoinette said. "That was the cow that suckled all the little calves, you see."

He didn't see.

"Whiskey," she said, "or do you think Joe Kennedy was the only Irish king crowned with barley?"

Her brother liked hotels so much he started buying them elsewhere, moving across the Delaware Gap to Manhattan where there were plenty of hotels for a man with cash enough to weather the Great Depression.

"It was like that game they played in those days," she said. "The one with the little man in his top hat and cane and all those red hotels."

"Monopoly," Noah said.

"There you are," she laughed.

For a while they sailed on a river of crystal light into a sea of dew.

"What's in any satchel is more than it contains," Antoinette said.

"What's that?" he asked. It was a riddle he knew.

"If you think you know anything of my brother after all that, you are mistaken," she mused.

"I know," he said and rowed under the stars for a while.

Antoinette Ryan hummed.

"There's a sprit sailing rig for this thing under the screen house," she said after a while, "which I didn't make you drag out."

"I thank you for that," he said.

She laughed. "Oh it's light enough I used to rig it myself. This seat comes out and the mast sits down beneath it. I used to sail her all over this lake. I was a friend to swans—they nest here, you know, mean things they are like most terrible beauties…"

Terrible beauty, Noah knew, was a phrase from poetry.

They lived with, and sometimes against, poetry, he knew, he and Liam. Liam had written an essay for his college applications which Cathleen could recite in the same way Antoinette recited how guide boats ride the waves like ducks. In it Liam located his heritage in language. From Noah he said he inherited a language of justice and from Cathleen one of music.

There was more to it, Noah knew. Liam had written something about how one of them made him strong and the other made him mindful of the weak. He couldn't remember it exactly—trained more to quickness than to memory—but it involved an important inversion—it was poetry which made him strong and law which made him mindful of weakness— and on the whole it was very touching, a consolation to them as he went off.

It was more than that: it was a great surprise, as if he had gone off to his room as a boy to play video games and then, seemingly just hours later, emerged as a full grown man, an actual prince with armor like a mirror.

Noah tried to think how it must feel to sail off away from your children as the Frenchwoman had, sailing off to a world of words. Men used to leave their families for war, Antoinette's aunt's sons had sailed off and become policemen in New York. Men ran away from their wives and wives drove away through the mountains and never came back.

He was remembering the French woman all wrong, his memory inverting it in recollection, concentrating on the cluster of hurts instead of how they had slipped through the waves of those nights like magic.

We have come to fish for the herring fish
That live in this beautiful sea

It was so sad really to remember anything. Antoinette's dead baby as soft as the moon.

"Why did you say your son is a moth?" Noah had asked the French woman.

"Ah, so you hear-ed this?" she asked, her question-fractured music.

What did she wear the second time? He tried to make his memory yield a color. The first night was a pastel cotton dress the color of daylight, the third—the awful and strange daylight meeting—she wore a white blouse and a simple straight skirt. She came straight from the library he remembered, stopping only for the pot of violets which she held before her like an absurd bonnet, the terra cotta pot against the white blouse, the splay of mottled foliage and the few pale violets.

The second time was a sequined leotard, Claire de Lune.

He saw the green skirt billowing in memory and she gathering it up and she squatting to relieve herself before he looked away.

"I dreamed him so once," she answered him, "a moth in a book like living paper. After the dream—he was just a baby then and I was afraid he would die like the other one—I became certain that I had always conceived of him thus. Even before his birth, I realized, in my imagination he was a moth. Sometimes what we know we cannot say without the word which only seems to come afterward but which has always been there in the knowing. This is what poetry is, *n'est ce pas?* I conceived my own son, I mean this word exactly. He was drawn to me as a moth is drawn to candles. I called him to me with words on fire."

They were stunned, no one had ever talked to them like this, not even their most histrionic English teacher.

"Why are you telling us all this?" Pete asked earnestly. "I mean it's almost a waste, isn't it?"

"So sweet…" she said and laughed. "My huge camel moth!

No words are wasted on you. You carry them over the dry desert in your hump."

She laughed and poured more wine into her paper cup.

"Perhaps the wine tells its own stories, *n'est ce pas?*" she asked.

N'est ce pas meant is it not. You asked whether something was other than what it was. It was the opposite of poetry Noah felt certain.

Sometimes he wished he could ask Cathleen what she was thinking, wished he could know not the word which formed the thoughts but the words which came along before them and which she passed over or rejected, fingering them like stones along a beach, feeling their heft and smoothness, tossing them back into the boil of water at her ankles.

That, too, he knew was poetry. He knew he had poetry within him, an artifact of marriage, something he possessed now as surely as dowry, not the poetry itself—that was his and truly within him—but the knowing it was there.

It was also a true memory, if there was such a thing. The boil of water at her ankles and the stones she fingered and then tossed back were actual memories, whatever that meant. It had happened along the lake shore when they first—or when he at least—fell in love and she was a girl in a saffron beach dress.

And the French woman wore a green dress, only a little lighter than the dark green of the pine trees. And the sleeping Antoinette wore sky blue Shaker cotton under the stars. And Cathleen—sleeping where?—wore only her white skin under the white sheets and sometimes in their bedroom the moon through the venetian blinds painted her cheek with three bars of light.

These facts were poetry and had their own justice.

Still he and Liam lived as much against as with poetry, he knew, not against like a battle but against in the way you lean against a door post unable quite to go through. Sometimes he wondered how Cathleen could stand it, what men they were. Third and two on the two with twenty seconds left, oh for six today on third down conversions in the red zone. Stop being weird; you stop being obstinate; I don't even know what that means; you'd know more if you spent more time studying and less on video games; you see how weird you are; you see how obstinate you are; whatever; not that again, I hate that fucking word; whatever.

Whatever. Whatever.

It had probably been like that for the French woman, he and Pete, the tight end and the forensics champ, two gaping boys steeped in testosterone and beer. It wasn't much different for Antoinette, the counselor and the satchel. There was a pattern here, what was a story if it wasn't that.

Whatever. They say angels come to you when the universe finds you wanting, he thought.

"What was in the satchel was the Cezanne," she said, answering the riddle.

"What?"

The image caught him unaware, for a moment he had an image of the canvas sewn into the lining of the suitcase.

"Mystery," she said. "Every container contains its own mystery besides its contents. It's what makes sex so interesting to the human species," she said.

"I *knew* there was something," Noah said and she laughed and then she recited again:

The old moon laughed and sang a song
   As they rocked in the wooden shoe,
And the wind that sped them all night long
   Ruffled the waves of dew.

"Edward Field," he said.

"Eugene," she said. "Even so, you catch on fast."

Their talk, even in the back and forth, was slow and easy like the rock and swell of the water they floated upon. They spoke nearly in whispers since the curve of the wooden boat held them in its sounds.

"I'm the old moon of the lullaby," she said. "You are indulging an old woman, Mr. Noah Williams, and that is very, very kind of you."

The truth was that he didn't think her an old woman except when she said something about lovers or sex or something else which made her flesh seem so unlikely. Otherwise, and this was a paradox, she had come this evening to seem more fully fleshed to him, more alive and womanly, than he ever had imagined possible for someone her age, than ever he would have thought her in the days when he saw her as a painted moon with circles of rouge on her cheeks.

He imagined that her riddle meant that the satchel itself was a receptacle of the wishes of the woman who had carried it, that her aunt had carried it like someone would carry her own dreams given half a chance, and that the Cezanne painting was no different, a container of dreams.

He tried to explain this as best he could.

"That's half of it," she said. "But half in this instance is twice enough. The rest has to do with the way dreams are drawn to other dreams, not unlike how clouds fold into one another like egg whites."

Still, as someone who lived against as much as with poetry, he couldn't help wanting to know certain facts.

"But where did the Cezanne first come from?"

"First and last from point X," she said.

She was yawning already, it was already past eleven he guessed and then was shocked to look down and see from the glowing dial on his watch that it was past twelve.

"We should go back in," he said. "You need your sleep."

"I've reached an age when I no longer sleep but watch the world with a rheumy eye. I stay awake with the moon," she said.

He was having trouble with words. He thought she had meant roomy, as if her eye had lots of room.

She laughed. "There's probably some truth to that," she said. "I'm increasingly wide-eyed as I get older. You get to a certain age and you can't really sleep any more and sometimes that's just as well because you don't really want to miss anything."

She sighed away another yawn.

"I wouldn't have missed this for anything," she said.

There was nothing to say so he rowed but the questions trailed behind them like the scalloped wake of the guide boat.

"What did you mean by X?" he asked after a while.

"Ah Noah, all the creatures two by two to the ark…" she said. "You are always the mathematician, aren't you? By this X, I meant an actual place, the X that marks the spot, beginning and end, alpha and omega…"

She smiled broadly. "Poor man, I fear you're always half afraid

I'm losing my mind. Listen to this: X in this case is the French for Aix-en-Provence, the place where Cezanne was born and where, alone in the end as I am, he came back to and painted your painting in there. Thus the alpha and the omega."

"But—"

"But you wanted to know," she interrupted his objection, "where and how did it first come to us, which isn't an X but a fifth, Fifth Avenue, where the fellow lived who owed my brother a lot of money, thirty thousand dollars as I remember it, unless I'm confusing it with the year in which he owed it and we acquired it, which was nineteen thirty I'm sure, two years after poor Liddie's death which was when Brian turned twenty-one and a man under the law although he was like too many boys who were already men then, having already worked himself so hard he looked like thirty at twenty-one and, having buried a wife and made a fortune, two years later by nineteen thirty looked like forty."

The numbers were like constellations, Noah knew, shapes of scattered lights.

"The fellow on Fifth Avenue said he couldn't pay and my brother slipped the painting off the wall and said 'I'll take this then' and the man said, 'But that's—,' and Brian said, 'Yes, it is, isn't it and that will do nicely,' and he stuck it under his arm and we were off."

"You were with him then?"

"Sure I was. I was with him always before Ryan and then after him and all the time before I went away to Spain when Rory died. Anyway Ryan and I were about to marry by then and my brother had thought at first he'd take the apartment on

Fifth for us to settle the debt but then he couldn't bear to put the old fellow out of his nearly empty home now that he'd almost lost it all."

She splashed water again, reaching over the side, her weight so slight the boat hardly tipped when she leaned over.

"I always did wonder whether my brother really did know what the painting was or whether it was just small enough to fit under his arm. In any case he gave it to me for my wedding."

She looked toward him across the dark boat.

"We're running out of stories, Mr. Noah, two by two…"

Once the French woman told them she spent her morning in the library looking at the notebooks of a famous writer who thought we were at the end of stories. They played the part of boys and asked, "How could we be at the end of stories?" and then "How could there be a book if there were no more stories?" And their questions had delighted her and made the night last. It all wove together too perfectly, Noah thought, rowing under the star showers.

It was past the Perseid season, Antoinette realized. "We're a week past it. July twenty-five to August eighteen is the formal season for them. How the year has gone on," she said. "You get a certain age and a year is a day and a minute is an hour. No wonder no one sleeps after a while. Still there will be stragglers if you look up toward the Perseids. There are always meteors, they are not something that falls on us but something we move through."

Noah let the oars rest and float and, like her, leaned back and watched the sky, directing his gaze toward the keyhole cluster of dim stars which she assured him were the Perseids. Almost instantly there was a comet streaking white across the night and decaying into a yellowing memory.

Stories were like this, he thought, they don't befall us, we move through them.

"*Ces questions exactement* are my concerns," the French woman had said. As the night wore on she had fallen more and more into a Francophone pidgin, "The end of stories is when they fell into language like the Chinese poet who fell in the pond looking for the moon. But the beginning of the book is when we first fall into language…which is, of course, when the baby comes from inside La mère and everyone is speaking…"

It was confusing for a young man. Confusing and a little exciting. He thought La mère was the sea.

"We arrive at the stories *comme les bébés*. I am reading these notebooks and letters here, and it is clear that stories begin and end, how do you say? in the warmth of the womb."

She laughed a little nervously, then yawned like a girl.

It was nearing morning there also.

"The love letters to his wife are all womb. Very sweet and naughty. These are kept under the key so no boys can see them, like the Playboy, *ne c'est pas?*"

It had been a little daring, the nearest she had come to what they might have imagined would happen if they spent the night drinking in some hidden place with a French woman. There was a thrill to how she teased them.

And do you write like this to your husband, they did not ask. She had said the children's father was god knows where and anyway she was much too real to them, too much there, to ever think of daring with her.

We were innocents, Noah thought, and she was a succubus. She was Lillith.

It was a story he enjoyed, Adam's other wife, the one who would not heed him and yet whom he slept with as soon as he was cast from the garden. It was "a parable of rectitude" according to Cathleen.

The opposite of succubus was incubus. If he could be an incubus he would sail through the night to where she slept, white under white sheets, sailing to her in an arc like a comet, streaking white across the night and never decaying. Burrowing in her like a worm, a whisper, the way a muscle tenses just short of cramping and then, warming, relaxes, lapses. Slipping over her like a cloud, oars through water, or a wife's memory of letters from her husband.

While she slept he slipped in and out of sleep despite himself. It was irresponsible. Irrational. Floating through the night with an old woman in his care, a client, a woman almost ninety, the moon already set, the two of them without life jackets or any other flotation device, without a reason or any history between them save this night.

He looked at citron shapes of scattered lights, the constellation of his wristwatch.

Four a.m.

Mrs. Ryan. Antoinette. We have to decide things.

Still she slept. There were comets in the corners of his eyes, birds beginning to sing.

Conservatively, a Cezanne like this could be expected to bring millions at auction. How many he did not know but her whole estate not worth much more than a million five, less the house if she insisted, as she indeed insisted, on giving it to the nature conservancy. The guide boat would be worth what?

A stupid question. He was dozing again. The boat was pocket change and so he knew that he had slipped from the calculations into a daydream. In dreams the value of things was disproportionate. A moth in a book.

He wondered if they rowed in whether he could lift her from the boat without tipping it, carry her up to the dark path to the twig sofa with the Hudson Bay blanket or, depending on how light she was, all the way up to the small room with the irises.

He scooped water from over the side and washed his eyes awake, his weight setting the small boat rocking.

When the bough breaks the cradle will fall and down will come baby.

The French woman's wife was a midwife. No, that was wrong. The French woman's mother. And the French woman was a mother, an earth mother, a moth's mother, a candle.

He scooped again and she woke with the rocking, waking like a kitten, scratching at her eyes and yawning without sound.

"O Mr. Williams," she said, "dear Mr. Noah Williams, what a gift you've given me," her yawning a dark O in the whiteness, "I haven't slept like that for ten years…"

Since her last lover he thought, on the Costa del Sol.

There was another story: How is it you were given a French name. And another: what happened to Mr. Ryan and why didn't you marry again.

We were orphans, my brother and I, orphans of history, doomed to live without issue. Liddie died of consumption despite what Rory spent trying to keep her breathing. He was only a boy though he looked like a man. Ryan was a commercial traveler who fell in love with a princess disguised as a house maid and once he had her I think he missed the road too much no matter how much he loved me. He drank himself away eventually, turned so yellow from the jaundice the children called him the Chinaman. Cirrhosis. Rory giveth and Ryan taketh away. God he was handsome though, before he turned yellow.

Stories were like this, we fall in and out of language, in and out of families. A parabola of curvature.

Mulvey? He snapped off like a light switch. The scarred heart gave out in a flash of darkness. His sister sailed off in a wooden shoe, setting off for the coast of Spain like the old songs.

Let me burrow in you like a worm, my love.

Claire de Lune spun on a thread like a sequin.

The story of how she got her name was a good one, she would come out of the dreams to tell it. Give her just a minute.

It was near morning and they were getting the boat out of the water when he remembered to ask her.

Even more than getting the boat out of the water, he was worried about getting her out of the boat. The boat could rest on its hawser, rising and falling with noon. She would need sleep and warmth and care.

But she was out of the bed before he'd tied it off. No, that was wrong. She was out of the boat before he tied it off.

It was an interesting slippage, boat and bed.

"I always found myself saying wedding for funeral," she said. "Even as a young woman—and well before I married Ryan, I must say—I mixed the two words up."

She was holding the boat against the dock for him, back bent all the way over like a hasp.

"I'm on the brink of speaking the word spry," he said.

"Just try it and I'll push you in," she said. "I tell you I haven't slept like this for ages. Maybe I should set off every night like Wynken, Blynken and Nod and let the boat rock me to sleep. If I died out there they could set me on fire like a funeral barge…"

She looked up at him and laughed, her palm against his chest.

"There's no them to set fire to it," she whispered. "I'd have to come back and set my own barge burning."

"Well you'll just have to try not to die," he said sincerely.

"Oh I do, Mr. Williams," she said earnestly, "I do."

"Noah," he said.

"I know," she teased.

He asked her then about her name.

"Seriously, we had better get the boat back under the screen house," she was saying.

"*We* will do nothing of the sort," he said. "I'll drag it up, you tell me about your name."

"Antoinette?" she asked, her voice delighted.

"Do you have another?"

"Millions," she said.

"Well then, you have lots to tell me, don't you?" he said.

The wet hull of the boat rode easily above the black and dew-wet grass as if it were sailing on invisible sails, gliding so swiftly she could not keep up with him as he pushed it and so he had it back under the house and nearly wrapped in the tarp again before she caught up with him, walking slowly up in the dark furrow the prow had made through the shadows.

When she reached him he realized he was out of breath from the push and bone weary now from the long night, so weary he could not stop yawning.

"Shall I make you tea?" she asked.

"No, I really have to go."

"You should get your painting then," she said.

"You know I never could."

"I know," she said.

"I've been thinking though," he said.

He said this in the way you suddenly say I've been thinking of something when you haven't been aware you have, just as suddenly saying it and knowing after all that you have been thinking it exactly in some other self. It made thought seem alien.

Even so it was she who said it, what he was thinking.

"Perhaps we should look after Liddie's line," she said. "My poor great-grand-nephew and his wife and their pickup truck and trailer."

"And baby," he said.

"Yes, that would be the point, wouldn't it?" she said. "We'll loan it to some museum in the interim but will it to the child when it comes of age. Do we know what kind this creature is, counselor? Girl or boy?"

"We can find out," Noah said.

"It doesn't matter really," Antoinette said dreamily, "though I wish it were a girl. It would make such a good story. A little girl comes of age and inherits a Cezanne."

"She could end up hanging it in her trailer, you know," he cautioned her. "It's a lottery."

"She could tear it from the frame because she liked the frame better. She could skim it over the water and watch it sink," Antoinette said. "It goes on and on, doesn't it?"

"You could play safe," he said.

"How? Donate it to some college for the edification of young men and women? They, too, could tear it from the frame or skim it on the water, isn't that so, counselor? We were orphans, my brother and I, orphans of history and once again we have to depend on an orphan's lot. We've done well enough once before, who can say we don't do well enough once again?"

"Let's think about it again in daylight," Noah said. "Another day, when you've rested and had a chance to think it over. I have to go home and wait for Cathleen."

"Yes, you do," she said. "Would you like to see the painting again before you go?"

He shook his head.

"A wise man," she said and took his arm and they walked slowly up the hill toward the house.

It wasn't the end. There was another story, the story of how she came to be named Antoinette. Pete Ehmer died in a car crash in Indiana in October and that wasn't the end either. Noah wondered if there was any way to let the French woman know. He kept thinking there was another meeting. Felt certain. Remembered or supposed, wished or imagined. Liam went away and would eventually come home, midterm break and Christmas, spring break and summer, at least the first year, then a weekend or a week, dwindling to occasional days, then, years later, back with his family, his own daughters. A son perhaps.

He would be a lawyer himself, a doctor, a poet, a painter, a carpenter, an anthropologist.

Anything could happen. It was a cliché but that didn't make it any less true.

Some things were certain. Certain memories were true. Stones rattled against each other in silence under the waves of oceans and lakes, the currents of streams. Stones nestled against stones in the smallest ponds.

Will we ever be done with the stories, he wondered as he drove home to her through the dawn. He knew she was driving home to him as well and he wondered if she was thinking this also.

He thought of the questions of mathematics which were called story problems and how at Liam's age they became a part of your life for a time, even a matter of intense concern, and then you did not hear of them again.

If a woman in a yellow dress were to leave a blue motel at six a.m. and drive northward at seventy miles an hour and a man in blue jeans and a grey teeshirt proceeded southeasterly at the speed of light just before dawn, what would happen to them?

Some things were certain even in the subjunctive. Cathleen would arrive in the thin milk light of earliest morning still smelling a little of her brief sleep in an alien bed. Whether they would make love or not, she would stand in the dim half-light across their room and slip from her clothing, stepping free of the skirt or slip or jeans, lifting the panties in a deft step over each successive foot, tossing the clothes away upon a chair or into the hamper. She would look a little shy, a little amorous, annoyed to find herself fleshier than she wished in mid-life and yet aware he found her voluptuous. She would move toward him half-smiling, both pleased and a little peevish on account of how he gazed at her, the copper aureoles above the white and ample breasts, the tuft of dark hair between white thighs threaded with the first silver. She would lift the sheet up in a billow like a sail, settling it over them again. He would press against her, he himself so much fleshier now, feeling his belly against her back, his knees folded behind hers. They would hold each other and moan for their lost baby, their son set sail across the mountains.

Eventually they would turn and find each other's mouths and gorge there, feeding on each other.

Eventually, because she was a poet, she would find words for it: husband and son, billow and mountains.

Eventually he would walk down to the wild edge and pull the weeds from the stones then change the spark plugs of the tractor and load the tools and drive the tractor and trailer back up. Later he would rub the tools with oil to keep them from rusting.

Perhaps one day they would have flower tea with Antoinette Ryan in the screen house and Cathleen would see the transparent and unfinished faded lapis lazuli of the landscape at Aix. Perhaps he would row them both out in the guide boat, or set out under sail, their hands trailing in the water.

Surely in days to come he would tell her everything he remembered of the French woman because he knew she would be hungry to know.

Surely one or the other would one day die and then there would be memories, sadness and joys which tugged against you like currents under water, like the click of stones beneath the silent water.